Bedeviled

Tori Minard

Bedeviled

Book 2 The Gage and Nova Trilogy
An Avery's Crossing Novel

Tori Minard

Enchanted Lyre Books

Chapter 1
Heartbreak

Nova:

Rays from the mid-day sun glared off the fresh snow in a blinding tidal wave of light. The bright, hard, pale blue of the sky formed a cold vault overhead, reminding everyone of winter's ruthless beauty—just in case we'd forgotten in the few hours since the last brutal snowstorm had broken. All around us rose mountains and hillocks of snow built up from the storm to remake the world, and the parking lot of Joe's General Store, into its own image.

The accumulated flakes sparkled in the light, mocking and falsely cheerful. Beneath my booted feet, the snow probably squeaked from the extreme cold but I couldn't hear it. I couldn't hear anything except the whoomp-whoomp of the chopper.

The wind created by the blades of the luxury helicopter which sat in the parking lot like some kind of alien visitation blew my long hair in a thousand different directions. It had to be the coldest, cruelest wind I'd ever felt, the breath of some evil winter spirit. It was taking the man I loved away from me.

The deep-freeze around me crept under the hem of my parka. It battered its way through my zipper and down the neckline of the coat, driven by the chopper blades. The cold bit into my flesh, sinking deeper with every rotation of the blades, until it invaded my bones.

My fingers were numb. My thighs, too. The wind slammed right through my jeans and even the thermal leggings I wore underneath, easily reaching my legs and turning them to ice. Even my fleece-lined boots couldn't keep my feet warm enough for this encounter.

The inside of the chopper was a mystery to me, but the aircraft was definitely enormous. It looked nothing like the small ones used by local news organizations to watch traffic. It didn't even resemble the rescue copters sent out by hospitals, and it was way too shiny, with its bright white and cobalt blue design, to look anything like a military chopper.

A craft like that didn't belong in Subalpine, Oregon. It originated in a world so far from mine it might as well be on another planet.

I thought I knew heartbreak. When I caught my now ex-boyfriend Barry cheating on me with my roommate, I'd thought my heart was broken then. But that had been nothing, just a minor ache, compared to this.

I crossed my arms defensively over my chest. The stench of aviation fuel soiled the pristine winter air. Gage, the man I'd foolishly fallen for, bent over in a running crouch, his brown hair flattened by that same icy wind, and ducked beneath the whirling blades with his usual grace and self-assurance. He'd clearly done that maneuver a hundred times at least.

This was the first time I'd ever been close to any helicopter, let alone one so fancy it looked like it could have transported a president or a king. Gage belonged to another world, a world to which I'd never have access. To him, luxury helicopters were an everyday occurrence. To people like me, they were a crazy intrusion of fantasy into our regular world, almost as weird as if Cinderella's coach had rolled into the parking lot.

I'd just told Gage I loved him, not that it made any difference in his behavior. He'd still headed right for the chopper without a backward glance. Why had I said that? I should have kept it to myself.

He never looked back at me on his way into the aircraft. Was it that easy for him to leave me? Granted, we hadn't known each other very long, but it had been a really intense eight days. I could never have walked away from him like that, as if it was just another routine action on a routine day.

I squinted into the brilliance of the sunny winter day. He shut the chopper door behind himself, disappearing from my view. With the door shut, I could no longer see him through the reflective window.

My heart squeezed itself into a tight, hard knot. I ordered the tears threatening to flood my eyes to go the hell away. Crying was out of the question. People—Marcia and Misty, Joe's wife and daughter—were watching. It was possible Gage was watching, too, and I didn't want him to see me break down.

He'd made it clear he didn't want my love, that he had secrets he could never share with me, that his life had no place for me in it. I'd never expected him to commit to a relationship with me—I knew better. That knowledge didn't spare me the pain of watching him leave, though. Apparently, nothing would.

The blades whirled faster, roaring, throwing snow into the air. I'd saved his life, pulled him from the freezing McKenzie River when he'd fallen in and nearly drowned. Then I'd nursed him through hypothermia and stomach flu. I'd done things for Gage that I'd never done for any other human being. But he was a famous actor whose life lay in Hollywood, not in some Podunk Oregon mountain town, and he could never have stayed with me. Even if he didn't have a dangerous secret he refused to share.

I turned my back on the chopper as it lifted into the air.

2

***

Gage:

From the air, the lights of Los Angeles at night seemed to mock me, their sparkling red and green and yellow pretending to a beauty the city didn't really possess. Darkness and light worked together to cover up the haggard lines of sleeplessness, poverty, and hard living that marred so many of its neighborhoods, the plastic fakery of the suburbs. In the night, and from a distance, the illusion seemed real and welcoming, a comfort after time spent away from home.

The minute I stepped off the plane and onto the boarding ramp, the warmth and stink of L.A. wrapped around me like a filthy old blanket, destroying the illusion of beauty. The air felt wrong—too dry—and smelled wrong—dirty, full of exhaust fumes, smog. The chemical stench of aviation fuel assaulted my nose.

The constriction of the plane gave way to the roomier surroundings of the boarding ramp, yet my team still surrounded me, hemming me in. People talked, laughed, shouted, some of them at my elbows and others too far away to understand what they were babbling about. Behind me, the flight attendants mechanically thanked escaping passengers for flying with the airline and wished them a happy stay in Los Angeles.

My feet, the feet of all the people around me, thumped along the floor of the boarding ramp, making hollow sounds that echoed the hollowness inside of me. That empty feeling had haunted me for a long time. Years. But somehow it had become even more acute, more cutting, than it had ever been before.

Other passengers looked forward, watching for the family members or friends who awaited them, who would greet them and welcome them. A real welcome, not one painted on with fancy lights over the cover of night. My welcome had stayed behind in Oregon.

I hadn't been out of town very long at all, yet everything had changed, especially inside of me. Somehow, being nearly drowned, then nearly dying of hypothermia, and afterward suffering with a brutal case of stomach flu all while being trapped in a cabin with a stranger had transformed me.

I wasn't sure exactly what I'd transformed into; I only knew I'd changed.

Cindy, my personal assistant, and several members of my security team flanked me so the expected crowds of fans couldn't get too close. The noise of them penetrated the boarding ramp. Somebody had found out when and where I'd be re-entering the city, and people had turned out to view the spectacle.

Let the mindfuck begin.

What would all those fans do, what would they say, if I told them I hadn't earned their admiration? If I told them my fame and fortune was all due to a deal with the devil, would they hate me? Would they turn around and go home?

Nah, probably not. A deal with the devil has got to be good for a juicy scandal and lots of trophy pix, right? Besides, nobody believes in the devil these days. They'd probably just think I'd fallen into the same drug trap that had killed my best friend and fellow actor Jeremy Lindstrom, that I was hallucinating or delusional or some shit.

If only.

The screaming, the click and flash of a hundred cameras, all hit me like a wall the second we emerged from the boarding ramp into the airport terminal. People—mostly females—yelled my name, questions about where I'd been, why I'd disappeared. I kept my head down and pretended to ignore them, while my security guys pushed their way through the crowd. In my peripheral vision, I saw a sea of the plastic-looking painted faces so common in this city, along with perfectly manicured female hands extending slips of paper for me to sign.

I did not want to be here. It was only professional and personal obligations that had forced me to come back. My heart was still in Oregon with Nova, and I couldn't even tell her that. She couldn't know how I felt about her or *he* might come and take her away forever. I'd rather be lonely and heartbroken than allow him to hurt Nova.

"Mr. Dalton is very tired," my head security dude said firmly. "He won't be signing any autographs tonight."

They hustled me downstairs to my waiting limo, surrounded with more clots of screaming fans and shouting photographers. Somehow, I got myself into the back seat of the car and shut the door on the madness. The tinted glass shielded me from the mob, cutting the noise of their hollering down to a manageable level. I tried to picture Nova in this situation and failed. She was so quiet, so natural and real. She would never fit into this world, and I wouldn't want her to try. She deserved better than this, and better than me.

God. What was I going to do without her? I'd become helplessly addicted to her in the few days we'd had together. That was not something I would ever have predicted, me falling for a girl so quickly, so completely. In fact, I would have said it was impossible, until it had happened to me. But I'd had to leave for her protection.

I was protecting her from this, from a world I didn't even want anymore. Nothing looked the same. SoCal was too bright, too warm, too crowded, too full of fucking exhaust fumes and strip malls and people who knew who I was. But I was also protecting her from the ugliness of a deal with the devil, and that was something we couldn't move away in order to avoid. It would follow us wherever I went.

"Welcome home, Mr. Dalton," the limo driver said.

"Thanks." I stared out the window as he pulled away from the curb.

Welcoming me was part of his job. He didn't mean it. He didn't not mean it, either. It was just something he said, the way the hostess in a restaurant wishes you a nice day when you leave.

Still, I felt the heavy irony even if he didn't. The eight days I'd spent snowed in with Nova Pennyman had changed me so much that L.A. didn't feel like home anymore. A suspicion kept sneaking into my head that my home was now with her, wherever she happened to be.

Unfortunately for both of us, I was not worthy of a relationship with her. Not with anyone, really, but especially not with a girl like Nova Pennyman. She was far better than I would ever deserve.

Home was a luxury condo I'd bought a couple of years earlier. I had no bags. They'd been lost, along with my rental car, when I'd abandoned it and fallen—drunk and high—into the McKenzie. If not for Nova, I'd be dead.

I walked, bagless, upstairs to my dark-gray bedroom. I wasn't dead, was I? No. Hollow, though. If you tapped my outsides, there'd be an echo inside me. I fell on my bed and stared at the ceiling.

The place felt empty. It was the best I could afford, and that was a lot of luxury condo, but my very breath seemed to echo off the hand-applied Venetian plaster I'd spent a goddamn fortune on. I didn't give a fuck about Venetian plaster. That was the choice of the designer I'd hired to decorate the place, because you know an A-list star needs an A-list home.

This wasn't a real home; it was a showcase.

No smell of woodsmoke, just the chemical stink of new paint and carpet. No battered old comfortable furniture, just ultra-modern minimalist sculptures too precious to actually use. No soft sounds of Nova moving around, working in the kitchen or sitting with her sketchbook or even hunched in the bathroom puking.

Fuck. I missed her. I even missed the sound of her being sick.

That was fucked up.

How could I miss someone so much when I barely knew her? We'd only been together a few days. Just a little over a week. Yet I felt connected to her in a way I'd never felt with anyone else.

If it were safe, I'd get on the next plane and go back to her. But I couldn't.

Leaving her was my way of being noble. Because I had a weight on my shoulders that I couldn't seem to shift, and I didn't want it to crush her. She meant too much to me.

The central truth of my life was that my mom made a deal with the devil when I was ten—my soul in return for fame and fortune as an actor. Sounds crazy, I know. But it's true. I was there and saw the whole thing.

That fucking Deal had both shaped and ruined my whole life. I had indeed become a highly successful actor at a ridiculously young age, and my career was still shooting upward. I had an obscene amount of money. I'd won an Academy Award for playing the role of a heroin-addicted rock star who self-destructs at the height of his fame and success.

All good things, right? Except I hadn't earned them. I'd been given my success, with my soul in hock. Supposedly, *he* was going to come for me at the height of my fame. I would die then, kind of like the heroin addict I'd played.

I didn't want to die. But I was more concerned about the people around me, people like Nova. Because my mom claimed that the devil had informed her he'd come after people close to me, if for some reason he couldn't get me after all.

Despite my best efforts, I'd fallen hard for Nova Pennyman. I couldn't stand it if something terrible happened to her and I'd do anything to protect her from my problems. Even if it made me miserable to do it.

Now that I was back in L.A., I was thinking I shouldn't have left her. I should have stayed with her and fought. I could've called in my security team to deal with the media bullshit. I'd run because...well, because it was a habit and because I didn't want Nova to get hurt because of The Deal.

That shit was going to stop. I would deal with The Deal, as soon as humanly possible. Like right now.

My life had been mostly going with the flow, letting my fate be determined first by my mother—when I was still just a kid—and then by that infernal situation she'd created. I'd let it, and the devil, own me. In fifteen years, I'd made no real attempts to fight, assuming it would be impossible.

No more.

I owed it to Nova to figure this shit out, make it right.

But how do you fight the devil?

Rolling off the bed, I padded over to my desk and my laptop. Powered up the thing. There had to be some kind of information on the Internet, something about supernatural agreements or deals. Right? Everything else was on the Web, so why not deals with the devil?

While I waited for the computer to boot up, I took out the drawing Nova had given me just before I'd left her and set it next to me on the desk top. She'd done it in pencil, making me sit still for a long time while

I stared out the window at the falling snow. At the time, I'd thought it was the most boring thing I'd ever done, and now I was glad I'd put up with it.

I had this drawing. The only piece of Nova I'd thought to take with me. We had no photos, no record of any kind of our time together. I'd never been a sentimental guy, but that fucking hurt. I wanted a picture of her to help me remember her.

Hours later I was hungry and tired of scrolling through page after page about Faust and blues guitarists who'd supposedly met the devil at some lonely crossroads. I wasn't learning anything new here.

See, that's long-standing folk tradition—if you want to learn some particular skill, especially in music, you go to the crossroads to call up Old Nick and strike a deal. My mom didn't go for that traditional stuff, though. She was all about convenience. If you're gonna call up the devil, just go ahead and invite him into your living room. I mean, why go out when you can get delivery?

The thing that repeatedly struck me as I read was that my mom had made The Deal but she'd used my soul as the bargaining chip. I didn't think she had the authority to do that. It would be like trying to use someone else's house as collateral when taking out a loan. But if that was true, why had the devil accepted The Deal? You'd think Old Nick would have a pretty good grasp of these matters.

Clearly, this problem was going to take more research than I could do over the Interwebz.

Chapter 2
Avery's Crossing

Nova:

My new apartment was new only to me. It must have been built sometime in the seventies, judging by the godawful, gigantic Mansard roof that dominated the structure and made it look like some kind of angular, mutant mushroom. Or more accurately, a whole row of mutant mushrooms, since the apartment was part of a single-story development with the units strung together like hideous beads on a long out of fashion string.

I could afford it. That was the irresistible magic of this place.

The door, a flat beaten-down brown, was missing some of its finish around the knob. The unit numbers were the stick-on kind, peeling around the edges. There were metal numbers screwed to the outer wall, as well, just in case I forgot where I was.

The landscaping looked good from a distance, the shrubs neatly trimmed. Up close, though, you could see that they'd been hacked off by someone who had no idea what he was doing, since the dead gray innards of the shrubs were exposed in some places, showing through the decimated green growth like bone exposed by a terrible wound.

The misty January rain, while it cloaked and softened the view, also deadened all the colors. The gray sky seemed to press into the inside of my skull. The rain clung to my face with a chilly, damp caress.

Inside, the place smelled musty, like dry rot, the pungent scent of the hacked-off junipers blocked by walls and window glass. I hoped I could cover that mustiness up with scented candles. Maybe keeping the windows open for a while every day would also help.

Avery's Crossing hadn't changed at all since I'd left, but I was a different person. No traitor roommate to steal my non-existent cheater boyfriend. No cabin in the Cascade Mountains as a retreat. Just this rainy, Oregon college town, a part-time job, and a cheap place to live while I took a couple of art classes and tried to figure out who the hell I was.

Funny. That's what I'd gone up to the mountains to do. I hadn't figured out a single thing, except that I loved Gage Dalton, an actor who didn't have a place for me in his fast-paced Hollywood life.

Finding a man floating in a half-frozen river isn't something that happens every day—or ever, for most people. When that man turns out to be one of the hottest young Hollywood actors, well, it can have a strange effect on your life. I hadn't even liked him at first, yet within the week I'd fallen in love with him.

And he'd climbed into a helicopter and flown away from me without a backward glance.

My mom followed me with a load of kitchen supplies as I wrestled the last box of books through the door of the apartment and set them on the crappy living room floor. Like I said, the apartment wasn't really new, just new to me. In fact, it was ancient and nasty-smelling, but it would do. It was cheap and small but in a safe neighborhood, and those things were important to me.

I didn't need Gage. Maybe I wanted him, but I didn't need him. I'd do just fine on my own.

"I think you're making a huge mistake," my mom said.

"I know you do." She always did. She'd been telling me this ever since I'd left the cabin to return to Avery's Crossing.

"You could be going back to Pioneer."

And finishing my pre-med studies, my degree in biology, rather than fooling around with painting classes at a lowly state university like Central Willamette. But Pioneer—being a doctor like her and my dad— was what *she* wanted for me, not what I wanted for myself.

"Mom, it's going to be fine. I just need some time."

She put her hands on her perfect, skinny hips and shook her head. "You're giving up a great career, and to do what? Work at a fast-food place? A department store?"

"The Unique Boutique." I'd already told her the name of the place twice.

She gave me an understated eye-roll. "What a name."

"They gave me a job. I don't care what they call their business if they pay me to work there."

Gage's personal assistant, Cindy, would have had some choice words about the boutique, its name, its probably—according to her— fashion-challenged merchandise, and me as its new employee. I didn't care what Cindy thought either. If I wasn't seeing Gage, I didn't have to put up with her self-important attitude.

Funny. I'd only met Cindy once, and I thought I knew her opinions about my job, my home, everything. Of course, she'd made her attitude toward me pretty clear from the first minute she'd seen me.

"If you go back to Pioneer," my mom said in a hopeful tone, "your dad and I will pay for everything."

"I'm not going back there. I'm not going to be a doctor."

She stared at me, apparently baffled. "I don't understand you at all. First the cabin and now this. What are you doing, Nova? Are you okay?

Are you in some kind of trouble? You know we'll help you with whatever it is. No matter what."

"I'm not in trouble, Mom."

I hadn't told her about Gage. First, I didn't think he'd want anyone to know. People on his end must have done some expensive work keeping the story from getting out, because I hadn't seen or heard a peep about it except that he'd supposedly rented a hotel room where he'd waited out the storm. In reality, of course, the storm—which had begun just as I discovered him in the river—had snowed us into my cabin after I rescued him and we'd spent those eight days together, getting to know each other in intimate detail.

The other reason I didn't tell her was because I didn't think she'd believe me. And besides, I didn't want to share it. I didn't want to share him or make the brief time we'd had together into some kind of celebrity sighting on steroids.

Denial can feel pretty good at the time, but when reality finally crashes in, you get even more pain and you get it all at once. I'd been in denial about what would really happen when the storm ended and what Gage would do, how he'd treat me. I'd known we couldn't stay together, but I hadn't truly faced it.

And then I'd stood in the snow in front of Joe's General Store and watched Gage get into that helicopter. He said he wanted to be with me, yet he couldn't be bothered to try. Supposedly his life was too dangerous for me.

At least he had a unique excuse, right? Instead of coming out and saying he didn't want to give up banging his fangirls and be exclusive with me, he made it seem like he had some kind of epic enemy waiting around to destroy anyone he cared about. I guess I could take a deep breath of relief, because obviously I wasn't on Gage's cared-about list.

After he'd left, I'd gone back to the cabin and packed my things. As soon as the roads were clear enough—which took a few days—I'd driven myself here to Avery's Crossing, where I'd rented a cheap room at a dive motel and called my parents and told them my new plan.

I was going to work part time, take a class or two, and try to figure out what the hell I wanted out of life. No, I didn't want to move back in with them. No, I wasn't going to come home for the holidays. I was living in Avery's Crossing by myself and I'd visit their house for Thanksgiving dinner. I couldn't take my mom's constant concern if I moved back home.

I hadn't told them that last part, but it was definitely on my mind.

So I'd gone up for Thanksgiving and then again for Christmas. The rest of the past six weeks, I'd been here by myself. Signing up for classes. Looking for a job. Finding this crappy apartment, moving just enough of my stuff in so I could survive while the rest of it sat around in the storage unit I'd rented when I'd moved out of the place I'd had with my ex-roommate, Skylar.

She was another person I hadn't seen in a long time. We'd roomed together, even though I'd been enrolled at Pioneer and she was going to Central Willamette. We'd gotten along great, until the night she'd screwed my boyfriend, Barry, on our living room couch. Guess she hadn't planned on me walking in on them. That was when I'd decided to take some time off school.

Some people do that by back-packing across Europe. I went off and lived by myself in my parents' old mountain cabin.

My dad appeared in the beaten-up wooden door frame. He'd taken a day off from his practice to help me move in here. My mom, too, and she'd let me know all day long what an inconvenience it had been. Canceled appointments. Patients who weren't getting the care they needed.

The funny part was I hadn't asked for their help. I'd just informed them what I was doing. They had volunteered to come down from Portland to do this.

"Honey, are you sure this is what you want?" my dad said.

"Yes, I'm sure." I pushed some stray locks of hair from my eyes and glanced around the room.

Boxes and boxes of my stuff nearly hid the ancient, brown shag carpet. That shag had to be at least thirty years old and probably a lot older. It was worn bare in spots. I hadn't informed my mom of the carpenter ants I'd spotted on a windowsill. That would not have gone over well.

The bathroom was tiny and had only a shower, no tub. The kitchen cabinets looked like they were made of plastic and fiberboard, and the heat came from a hideous metal contraption in the living room that made a roaring sound and smelled like burning dust whenever I turned it on. But the rent was low and I thought I could afford to stay here a while on my savings.

My mom curled her nose. "You could at least have waited for us to help you pick out a place. This one smells."

It did smell musty. And like burning dust. "I can afford it."

She sighed. You know the one. The Sigh, always accompanied by The Significant Glance.

"Hey," my dad said. "How about we go see a movie and get some dinner before your mom and I go home?"

"Sure," I said. "Why not?"

An hour and a half later, I sat in the darkness of the theater, surrounded by the smell of popcorn and fake butter, the crunch and rattle of the audience gobbling their treats, and stared at the opening credits in disbelief. The movie starred Gage Dalton. Really? He'd had a new movie coming out the whole time he'd been with me and he hadn't said a thing.

I guess I should've paid more attention to the posters as we walked through the theater lobby, but I hadn't cared enough. I really only went to the thing because my dad had suggested it and I wanted him to feel like he was making me feel better.

Now, as I gazed up at the screen, Gage's image overwhelmed me. The square jaw, the huge blue eyes, the curly brown hair, the dimple in the chin, the graceful swagger of his walk. The muscular, male body that showed clearly through the close cut of his character's clothes. He was so beautiful he almost didn't look real, yet at the same time the hugeness of the picture made him seem super-real, ultra-real, more real than real life. Like I said, overwhelming.

It was a crime drama and he played the young, idealistic police detective. I couldn't take my eyes off the screen. God, he was good. Like, award-winning good. He gave a character that could have been nothing more than a string of clichés depth of feeling, of meaning, that I'd rarely seen. The subtlety of his expressions, of his voice...

Okay, so I'm not exactly a film critic. I hadn't seen all that many movies at that point in my life, at least not compared to some people. And I wasn't exactly unbiased, either. But I could tell good acting, and his was good.

When he was with me, he'd claimed he didn't deserve his fame and that anyone could do his job as well as he did. I hadn't understood the guilt and self-loathing I'd heard in his voice then and I didn't understand it now.

How could he say his work wasn't art?

If I'd had his number, I would have called him right there and chewed him out.

Then it hit me. I'd made love to that man. The young god up on that giant screen had held me against his naked body, kissed me, come inside me with my legs wrapped around his waist. I'd told him I loved him.

And then he'd climbed into a helicopter and disappeared from my life.

A tidal wave of grief and yearning rose up and swallowed me before I even noticed it coming. I wanted him back, goddamn it. I hadn't had enough, not nearly enough of him, his passion, his humor, the music he loved to play.

Suddenly I couldn't bear to look at the screen. I bent my head and propped my hand against my temple, struggling against tears and a crushing weight inside myself.

He was gone. We'd only been together a handful of days, but it felt like more. It felt important and real and he was gone.

I was being silly and I knew it. Gage had been out of my life for six weeks, almost five more weeks than he'd been in it. And my parents were with me. Now was hardly the time to break down and get all weepy over a guy who'd never been meant for me in the first place. But knowing didn't make the feelings go away.

Maybe what I felt for him wasn't love at all. Maybe it was only infatuation. But whatever it was, it was strong. So powerful I wasn't sure I could continue sitting here. Not with his voice, his face, his body all over that screen.

"Nova, are you all right?" my mom said in my ear.

"I'm fine," I whispered back.

"You don't look fine."

I stifled a sigh of frustration. "I've just got a headache."

"Do you want to go back to the apartment?"

"No. I'll be okay in a few minutes."

She gave me a lingering stare. I smiled faintly back at her. It was a fake smile and she could probably tell, but it was the best I could do. On screen, Gage was arguing with his partner. No, his character was arguing with his partner.

"All right," she said, and turned to watch the movie.

His voice flowed over me, deep and smooth and persuasive. All of this had been filmed long before I met him, of course, and had nothing to do with me. Yet a part of me didn't know that.

A part of me really felt as if he were speaking to me, somehow, through the medium of the screen. Which was flat-out crazy. It almost seemed as if he were there with me, yet at the same time he felt infinitely far away.

I would probably never see him again. All I would have of him was a few memories from our time in the cabin and this—this strange near-connection via a movie screen. It wasn't enough. It would never be enough.

Sitting here, watching and listening to him, was breaking my heart. It was worse than nothing, to see him this way.

I stood up and squeezed my way out of the row of theater seats. My mom got up too, following me. She'd want an explanation, of course, and I wasn't sure I could give her one. I certainly wasn't using Gage's name.

When I got to the end of the row, I broke free and stumbled down stairs flanking the amphitheater-style seating, making for the door, guided only by the colored bands of light set into the floor. My mom caught my hand, trying to stop me. I shook my head and kept going until I'd gotten all the way down and escaped into the access hallway.

"Nova, what on earth is going on?" she said as we neared the door.

"Nothing. I don't feel good. I'm sorry. I don't think I can finish the movie."

She peered at me through the theater gloom. "You don't look very good, actually."

"Gee, thanks, Mom."

"Do you feel feverish? Neck pain? Sore throat?"

"None of those. I'm just really tired. Exhausted."

My dad came up behind her, looking worried. "Is everything all right?"

"I'm going back to my apartment," I said. "You guys can finish the movie if you want."

"No," Mom said. "We'll take you home. I want you to be safe."

Good grief. I wasn't ten years old anymore. I almost rolled my eyes at her, but thought better of it at the last moment.

"If you insist," I said. "But it's not necessary. I'll be fine."

"You're not fine. You feel sick and you've been behaving strangely lately."

"Mom. I'm fine. Just tired is all." I forced another smile for her benefit. "I'm not used to all this excitement. I've been a hermit for months, remember?"

She pursed her lips. "I told you hiding out in the cabin wasn't a good idea."

"Yes, you did and you were right. Feel better now?"

Her lips puckered even more tightly. "Honestly, Nova. I don't know what to say to you anymore."

That made two of us. I didn't know what to say to myself either.

Chapter 3
Quest

Gage:

Smog hung over the city, although the snow-capped San Gabriel mountains were barely visible above the brownish haze. I'd never paid much attention to those peaks before, and now they only reminded me of Nova and her cabin. That was where I wanted to be, not here.

Daylight exposed all the wrinkles and age spots of the city that the night hid. The smell was even worse, the air dead with exhaust and wracked with city noise. Jackhammers, vehicle engines, car alarms, people shouting, a siren in the distance.

Grit and trash washed up in all the crevices and corners of pavement and sidewalks and buildings. A thick coating of garbage. The painted ho from the night had morphed into a shambling extra in a zombie flick.

I'd been searching for a way to get out of The Deal for a few weeks now and coming up empty-handed. No-one seemed to take deals with the devil seriously, at least not on the Internet. Either they thought it was a joke or they advised that a person in that situation should turn to God.

It might sound crazy, but I wasn't sure I believed in God. Not in the loving, protect his people from all harm sense, anyway. I mean, he hadn't protected Jeremy, had he?

As far as I was concerned, I was on my own.

There had to be someone who knew something, though. If I couldn't find knowledgeable people on the Web, maybe I could find some locally. There were all kinds of oddball people in L.A.

Today I had a couple of occult stores to visit. I'd never been to either of them, so it should be interesting.

I've never been one to have security following me around everywhere. Yeah, I brought them to that clusterfuck of a house party in Central Oregon, the one that had led me to falling drunk into a storm-swollen river, but on the whole I'd rather be on my own. Which made it a simple thing to drive over to a local occult bookstore to do a little research without my security dudes hanging on and finding out what I was up to.

I had this relatively nondescript car I used for jaunts like this, a gray Ford Fusion. Not flashy. Not a movie star ride, just a boring medium-gray sedan like most of middle America drives every day. That plus baggy clothes, a three-day growth of beard, and a baseball cap pulled low would, if I were lucky, keep anyone from noticing me.

In my wallet, I carried a tiny picture of Nova. I'd found it on-line. Some college friend of hers had posted a pic of her on a social media site and I'd snatched it for myself. A picture she'd given me herself would have been better, but this blurry little image was better than nothing.

When I looked at it, her smiling brown eyes seemed to look right inside of me. Stupid. She hadn't even known me when the picture was taken.

What was I going to do if I ever got to the place where I could reunite with her? I knew virtually nothing about long-term relationships. I showed more commitment to my mechanic than I ever had to any woman.

Hell, I wasn't getting anywhere with all this rumination. Just driving myself nuts.

The first store on my list was called Star Light Bookstore and Gifts. It lived in a strip mall, right between a shabby second-hand clothing store and a Mom and Pop bagel-and-coffee place. Funny location for a shop that sold occult supplies. I'd expected something a little more atmospheric, but this was Southern California, land of strip malls, after all.

Inside, the overwhelmingly sweet odor of Nag Champa incense filled my nose, making me want to sneeze. I recognized that smell from all the people I knew who used it to cover the reek of pot smoke. Never really worked, if you asked me.

An Eastern-sounding track full of twangy sitar and some kind of exotic flute played in the background as I wandered along display shelves crammed with wooden Buddhas and Tibetan prayer flags. Okay, so maybe this place was more New Age and less occult than I'd thought.

I turned around to see another shelf full of brightly painted statues of a fat guy with an elephant head. Weird. I'd seen statues like that around, mostly in Indian restaurants, which had given me the vague idea they represented a Hindu god, but I had no idea which one. Krishna, maybe?

"Are you a devotee of Ganesh?" said a dreamy female voice.

I turned. The owner of the voice looked to be about my mom's age, with close-cropped brown hair and a long, flowing dress with cosmic blue and purple swirls all over it. A huge silver pendant in the form of the om symbol hung on a chain around her neck. You see a lot of these New Age slash Buddhist slash whatever is fashionable at the moment people in the L.A. area, and I'd hung around with a few in the business, but I didn't know any of them very well.

"Who?" I said, clueless.

"Ganesh." She pointed to the elephant-headed dude. "In Hinduism, he's the remover of obstacles."

"Ah. Uh, no, I'm not a devotee." She'd probably already figured that out.

"Well, in that case, can I help you with something else?"

"Um...maybe," I said, suddenly self-conscious. "What do you know about the devil?"

She frowned vaguely. "The devil? Are you serious or in here playing a prank?"

"I'm totally serious."

The lady stared at me for another moment, her New Age serenity looking a bit frayed at the edges.

"Honestly," I said. "I can see why you'd think I was playing you, but I'm not."

"Your aura does look a little muddy," she said, "but I don't see anything really dangerous in it."

"That's a relief," I said, wondering briefly if she could detect the dryness in my tone. I was trying to keep it under control, but this place seemed to bring out something in me I didn't like.

"The devil is just a state of mind," she said, smiling serenely. "Don't give it any power over you and it can't harm you."

"You really believe that?"

Her smile never wavered. "Yes, I do."

I didn't. I'd seen the harm *he* could do, and if he was just a state of mind then how come he'd fully manifested in my mom's old living room?

"I don't know," I said uneasily. "I'm looking for something more concrete. Some kind of protection."

"We do have all kinds of crystals, which are powerful protectors against negative energy." She gestured toward glass display cases near the cash register. "Would you like some help choosing one?"

"Uh..." Crystals, huh? Somehow, a pretty rock didn't seem like it would be enough to stop the Prince of Darkness.

The lady stood there looking at me hopefully and I figured what the hell, it couldn't hurt. So I let her sell me a big chunk of smoky quartz and a piece of black tourmaline, which made her happy but didn't do much for me.

Supposedly, the crystals would absorb or deflect "negative energy" and keep "the devil" from harming me. As she spoke, I could almost see the quotation marks around the words "the devil", letting me know she didn't believe he was my real problem. Did she think I was nuts or just misguided? Not that I cared. I was outta here.

I left the rocks in my car when I went into the next place on my list, an establishment called Waning Moon. This one was a lot more like what I'd hoped for, being all dark and mysterious looking and housed in an old building from the twenties. Weird-looking curios crammed its front windows, everything from deer antlers and uncut crystals to exotic carved wooden boxes and an antique Ouija board.

A string of bells tinkled when I opened the door. This place also smelled like incense, but I couldn't place the exact scent. It wasn't Nag Champa, that was for sure. It seemed darker somehow.

The air seemed thicker in this place, too. Not ominous, like Jeremy's apartment had been when I'd found his body, but definitely heavier than normal. There was an odd sense of pressure on my skull, while the hair on the back of my neck prickled.

I glanced around at the displays of merchandise, but didn't see any clerks. It looked like I was the only person there. I wandered over to some dark wooden bookshelves, which sported titles like *Three Books Of Occult Philosophy* by Cornelius Agrippa and *The Book Of Abramelin The Mage,* along with some more contemporary books. None of them seemed to have anything to do with weaseling out of deals with the devil, though. They were more along the lines of achieving tremendous wealth and curing disease, although Abramelin did promise to teach me how to contact my Holy Guardian Angel.

I stared down at the odd little book. Was this for real? Did any of it work?

On flipping through it, I discovered that the process of meeting my angel was supposed to take an entire year and it involved fasting, celibacy, and a whole bunch of prayer. A year. I didn't know if I could wait that long, and besides there was no mention of the angel helping people get out of ill-advised deals with Lucifer.

A giant needle seemed to be stabbing me in my eye socket. I rubbed the orbital bone, grimacing. The only thing I'd accomplished so far was to give myself a headache. This occult shit was more complicated than I'd realized.

The rest of the store was filled with artifacts I mostly couldn't identify, let alone figure out how to use. Dried herbs in dusty jars, plastic baggies, and bundled into stick-like arrangements. More crystals, jewelry of all kinds—many pieces featuring dragons, pentacles, and other occult symbols—plus rows and rows of all kinds of strange, carved things. Tiny statues, candles shaped like naked people and human skulls, rows of miniature bottles of oil named neroli, rose geranium, myrrh...Whoa. Myrrh was real? I'd always thought that was some kind of made-up, mythical shit.

"Are you finding what you're looking for?"

I turned around, but this was no pleasant-faced New Age lady. This guy had one of the longest beards I'd ever seen, along with flat, secretive brown eyes that looked right through me.

"Sure," I said.

"That's a long process," he said.

"Huh?"

He pointed at my hand, where I still held the Abramelin book. "The Holy Guardian Angel operation. Takes over a year."

"Yeah. I noticed that. Does it work?"

He grinned, a startling expression in contrast with the former flatness of his eyes. "No idea. I've never tried it. Don't have the patience."

"Hmm." I stared down at the book for another moment.

"You need an angel?" the guy said.

I glanced at him, not sure if he was making fun or serious. He looked somewhere in the middle.

"It sure wouldn't hurt," I said. "But I'm not sure even an angel could help me."

"Sounds serious."

I snorted. "Yeah."

"Can I help?"

He didn't seem like the kind of guy who would help just out of the goodness of his heart. Those flat eyes made me uneasy. On the other hand, he was a salesperson in an occult supplies shop, so helping was his job.

I reached up with my free hand and tugged at the brim of my cap. "What do you know about deals with the devil?"

The guy rocked back on his heels, looking thoughtful. "The devil. Well, from my perspective, the devil is just a thought form."

"A thought form? What's that?"

"It's basically an entity that was formed and is maintained by the beliefs of humans."

I frowned. "So you're saying the devil doesn't really exist?"

"Oh, he exists. It's just that people invented him."

My frown deepened and I shook my head slowly. "That's the weirdest idea I've ever heard. I don't know if I can get my head around it."

It didn't seem very plausible. Could a human-created creature be as badass and powerful as the thing my mom had called up?

"It's a basic occult concept," the guy said.

"Can you protect yourself from a thought form?" I said.

"Yeah, sure you can. You just have to believe it's possible."

That sounded kind of lightweight, considering we were talking about the devil here. Plus I wasn't convinced about the thought form thing. He sure hadn't felt human-created when he appeared in our living room. All in all, what this guy was saying sounded pretty much like what New Age Lady had said, only in slightly different terms.

It's all in your head, son. Just think yourself happy.

There had to be better information out there somewhere and I was going to find it.

"Okay, well, I'll keep all that in mind," I said. "Thanks for your time."

He narrowed his eyes as he studied me. "You look familiar. Haven't I seen you somewhere?"

Time to go. When people started thinking they recognized me, they were just one or two steps away from figuring out who I really was.

"Uh, I doubt it," I said lightly. "I get that all the time. One of those nondescript faces, you know?" I laughed and put the book down on a nearby shelf. "I've got an appointment. Gotta run."

I left without looking back, hoping the guy didn't figure out who I was and then text everyone he'd ever met with the information.

Of course, if news got out that I'd been seen in an occult bookstore, I'd just pass it off as research for a role. Or something.

The air felt pleasantly warm against my skin as I left the shop. My denim jacket was getting too warm for the weather. This is SoCal in January. You never know whether you'll get snow or heat, but usually it's somewhere in the mild and bland category.

I was craving snow.

I shook my head at myself. Who wishes for snow and ice over sunshine and shirt-sleeves? Crazy people, that's who. People who scour L.A. looking for a way to cheat the devil.

Knots of people strolled the sidewalk outside the store, stopping to look into the window display of the pawn shop next door and the Asian grocery a few doors down. The haze seemed even thicker than when I'd entered the place. It made my eyes sting and itch.

I stepped out from beneath the dusty black awning into the dusty sunlight. Brick, stone, and stucco buildings lined the street. In the distance, a row of coconut palms lifted their heads into the smog.

As I headed back to my car, I noticed a man standing on the corner of the street, the one I planned to turn down on my way back. The only reason I noticed him was because he was staring at me. A fan? Paparazzi? He seemed a little too flashy for a pap.

The dude wore an elegant black suit that looked more like it belonged at the Oscars than a seedy L.A. street in the middle of the day.

And he was smoking a cigarette. The ciggy put off a lot more smoke than any other I'd ever seen, yet somehow his gaze—fixed on me—bored right through the clouds. The smoke smelled odd, too, not like regular cigarette smoke. It was sweet and spicy, almost offensively pleasant.

Something about the guy made my skin prickle with uneasiness. He was too focused on me and too out of place in this neighborhood. Old Nick might have sent him.

Should I confront him or avoid contact? If he was a watcher for the devil, then I didn't relish talking to him. And if he was a paparazzo, I'd only encourage him by initiating a conversation. Besides, I didn't need the bad press that would result from my punching another pap, even if the bastard had deserved it for getting physical with my date.

Those assholes can get into your personal life, spy on you, follow you around, even get into the intimate personal space of your female companion, and get away with it. But God forbid you should lose your temper and take a swing at one of them, no matter how provocative they're being.

I glanced around in my peripheral vision for an alternative to taking that corner. On my left was an alley leading between the shop building and the one next to it. My car was parked the next block over, so I turned into the alley as a shortcut.

High brick walls rose on either side of me, casting deep shadow over the alley. The rank smell of garbage fouled the air just a few yards in. Gravel filled the holes in the pitted black-top, crunching under my feet as I negotiated past a couple of stinking trash cans.

Was flashy suit guy going to follow me in here? I glanced over my shoulder, but he was nowhere in sight.

On the other side of the cans, a man sat cross-legged on the filthy pavement. He wore baggy pants that looked like they'd been khaki once, along with at least three shirts layered one over the other, and a sagging blue knit cap. Dirt smeared his craggy face, settling into the lines around his tired brown eyes and bearded mouth. He had a guitar on his lap.

I stared down at him for a moment, surprised by the musical instrument. It was an acoustic, kind of like the one Nova had at the cabin but better, and a whole lot bigger, a dreadnought style. I couldn't tell how much better it was than hers, since I hadn't heard it played yet, but there was something about it. When I looked at it—I can't really explain it. There was something about the lines of it and the way the pale wood of the soundboard gleamed that told me this was an extremely high quality instrument.

"You want a guitar?" he said in a rusty voice.

"Do you play?" I said, wondering where a guy like him would acquire a guitar of any kind, let alone one that looked like serious quality.

"Nah."

I frowned. "Where'd you get that?"

"Found it yesterday."

"You found it," I said, heavy sarcasm in my tone.

His eyes widened. "I didn't steal it. No way. I'm not a thief. I just found it laying around over there." He pointed across the alley at a small niche in the brick wall of the building opposite.

"Okay," I said.

He'd totally stolen it. How else would a guy like him end up with something like that? Or maybe someone else had jacked it and then abandoned it for some reason. Either way, it had to be hot.

The guy held it out to me with both hands. "Here, you have it. I don't want it."

I almost reached for it before I thought better of it. "Not a good idea. How do I know it isn't stolen?"

"It's not. I told ya."

"Yeah, but maybe someone else stole it. Maybe that's why it was laying on the ground." For all my reluctance, my hands were still partly outstretched. Because I wanted that thing. My fingers itched to feel its strings beneath them.

"Nobody would leave anything really valuable around here," he said, nodding wisely. "I oughta know. I've been hanging here for a long time and this is the first thing I've found besides old cigarette butts and a few quarters."

"Then how did it get here?" I said.

"Don't know. But I know it isn't stolen."

That made zero sense. He was probably high or drunk, making up stories and telling them to me because I was the only person around to listen.

Despite my doubts, my hands reached out a little farther. They wanted the damned thing and they didn't care if it was hot either.

"Come on, G," he said. For an instant, his eyes looked blue instead of brown. "It was meant for you. Besides, you'll play it better than I ever would."

I started. "What did you call me?"

"G. Is that what I said?" He blinked, looking confused. "Don't know why I said that. What's your name, anyway?"

"It doesn't matter." I grabbed the guitar. Then I reached into my pocket, pulled out my wallet and got him a stack of twenties. "You look like you could use this."

"Thanks, man." He tucked the money into the breast pocket of one of his under-shirts. "Real nice of you."

"Yeah. Uh, thanks for the guitar."

Only Jeremy had ever called me G. No-one else. Not our mutual friends, not the girls I banged, nobody. Only Jeremy. And his eyes had been blue.

I shivered as I carried the guitar down the remaining length of the alley, thinking idly that I'd have to buy a case for it.

That had been some freaky shit back there. I didn't know what to make of it. Maybe I'd imagined the eye-color change. I mean, that couldn't really happen, so it must have been all in my head. Didn't feel that way, though.

Was Jeremy trying to get in touch with me? Did he want me to have the guitar, and if so, why? Did it have some kind of esoteric power?

Hah. Right. A magic guitar.

If there were something magical about it, you'd think I would feel it when I touched it, but there was nothing. It just felt smooth and cool, like a normal guitar. The strings were all metal, and they felt exactly like normal guitar strings. Nothing unusual there as far as I could tell.

It's just a weird coincidence. Homeless guy finds an expensive guitar and tries to give it to the first person he comes across. End of story.

That was the normal, real-world explanation, but for some reason I didn't believe it.

I drove home, still puzzling over the whole incident. L.A. traffic being what it is, I had plenty of time to puzzle. Didn't really get anywhere though. I was just running around in circles inside my head.

I took the guitar and the crystals into my living room and sat down with them on my sleek, ultra-modern gray couch. I'd agreed with my decorator that I wanted this condo to have a masculine vibe, and the next thing I knew she'd made everything shades of black and gray. It was like the grayscale fairy had waved her magic wand of dullness over the place. But at least there weren't any crystal chandeliers.

I knew the guitar would need to be tuned, since it hadn't been played in a while. I gave the strings an experimental strum anyway, expecting to cringe at the sound.

It was perfect.

Perfectly in tune. How was that possible? The homeless dude hadn't tuned it. He didn't even know how to play.

Frowning, I started a melody, just something chosen at random to see what would happen. And damn if that guitar didn't have the prettiest voice I'd ever heard, full and rich and clear.

Was it really a coincidence that I'd come across this—this gift right after I'd struck out at two occult stores, while looking for a solution to my devil problem? I just couldn't see how a guitar could help me in that department.

At the moment, though, it was enough to feel and hear the music coming out of it. A sense of profound peace came over me as I finished up the first song and began the second, deeper even than my usual settling-in whenever I played. Maybe it was the pure sound of the thing, or maybe it was some other quality I couldn't identify, but this guitar felt different.

In movies, magical power is always really obvious. Things glow or jump around or talk directly to the hero or heroine. Or there are lightning bolts. I didn't have lightning bolts, though. I just had this bone-deep sense that everything would be all right as long as I could keep playing. Of course, nobody can play forever.

I had to break for dinner.

Half a leftover pizza later, I was back with the guitar. It was like a compulsion, this weird drive to play absolutely everything in my repertoire.

When I'd run through all the songs I knew, I started noodling around with a new piece. I had notes, riffs, in my head and they had to find an outlet before my skull exploded.

After some time experimenting with the new tune, I had to get up and find some staff paper before I lost what I'd composed. I've never been great at keeping new compositions in my head for more than a few hours.

It was a song for Nova. I didn't have the words yet, but I knew it was about her. And me. The way she made me feel.

I couldn't have her; not yet. Not until I'd resolved this devil bullshit. But I could write songs for her, and maybe someday she'd forgive me for walking out on her and not calling. Maybe someday we'd get together again and I could play the songs for her and she'd understand. I wanted that.

I just hoped she'd wait for me.

Chapter 4
Skylar

Nova:

I left Fairchilde Hall, the art building where I had my watercolor painting class, in a blinding glare of sunlight. My portfolio banged against my jeans-clad leg as I bent my head against the sun, carefully navigating the old, warped front steps of the building, which had once been a Victorian house. Even the overhanging giant spruce tree and the overgrown deciduous azaleas surrounding the front entrance couldn't block all the brilliant light from my eyes.

The sun shone, a rare event in January in Avery's Crossing, and I was depressed anyway.

The Willamette Valley is notorious for the amount of rain it gets in the winter, and the gray days can get hard to deal with, especially when you've had a couple of weeks of nonstop wet. When the sun shines, though, winter can be as beautiful as summer. To me, anyway.

I love the shapes of winter-bare trees, the way their structure is revealed when the leaves are gone. I love the lacy shadow-patterns they make across the emerald-colored grass. I love the pale, hard blue of the sky. There's something so energizing about a sunny winter day.

So why was I so down on this particular sunny day? I hadn't seen Gage in weeks. I was over him, right? Sure. Totally over him.

But as I hauled my huge portfolio and tool case full of painting supplies to my bike—it was easier to bike around campus than drive a truck and hassle with parking—I realized I still missed him. Still thought about him. Still drifted off into erotic daydreams about him whenever my attention wandered, and it wandered a great deal. Was I ever going to truly get over him?

He'd never called me. I'd given him my number. He could have called, and he'd chosen not to. Clearly he'd moved on, probably the instant he'd boarded that helicopter. I needed to do the same.

You might think I should take the initiative and do the calling, but I figured he must be bombarded constantly with fans' attempts to get close to him. His people wouldn't let me through to speak to him unless he'd given special orders about me. And since he hadn't come looking, it seemed unlikely he'd left those orders. Once he'd flown away from Subalpine, he was done with me.

I sighed and shifted the awkward weight of my portfolio. It wasn't especially heavy, just big. I was taking a watercolor painting class, and I had to carry a large drawing board and giant sheets of watercolor paper with me every time I attended.

The portfolio slipped out of my grasp and sprawled on the sidewalk.

"Damn it," I muttered, bending down to retrieve it.

"Here, let me help."

I froze at the sound of that so-familiar female voice. I lifted my head and stared at my former roommate as she picked up my portfolio.

"Hi, Skylar," I said dryly.

"Nova." Her brown eyes met mine, wide and wary. "How are you?"

"Oh, I'm great. Just great. I didn't expect to see you today."

"No, I—well, yeah, I mean —" She blushed. "I didn't either."

I held out my hand for the portfolio. "Still majoring in boyfriend theft?"

Her blush deepened and her gaze dropped. "I'm sorry about that. Really sorry, Nova."

"Don't be. I'm glad to be rid of him."

"We're not together. Barry and me, I mean. It was just that one time."

Did she expect me to be happy about that? Maybe part of me was, spitefully, happy that whatever they'd had was brief and meaningless. But the rest of me just couldn't get excited enough to care. Gage had completely supplanted Barry in my heart.

"Yeah," I said after a long, awkward pause. "Whatever."

"You don't care?" Her brow wrinkled. "I thought you and Barry were so good together."

"Is that why you fucked him?"

She recoiled. "Jeez, Nova!"

"Just wondering," I said with a shrug. "I honestly couldn't care less at this point. It was only casual curiosity."

Her eyes narrowed on me. "You've changed. Where have you been, anyway? You never returned any of my texts or emails. What happened to you? It was like you disappeared."

I'd changed, huh? Did that mean I no longer had "doormat" tattooed on my forehead?

"I took some time off school, that's all." I hoisted the portfolio. "Look, this is heavy and I need to go. I'll talk to you later, 'kay?"

"Oh." She looked disappointed, which surprised me. "Do you have to go right this minute? I thought maybe we could go for coffee or something."

I waffled. I didn't have a work shift at the boutique today, so I didn't have that excuse, but I really didn't know if I could forgive Skylar for what she'd done.

"I guess I could take a half hour or so," I said.

"Great!" She beamed and held out a hand. "Let me take some of that. We can go to the M.U."

I handed her my toolbox. As soon as she grasped it, her hand dropped to her side with the weight of the box.

"Wow, this thing really is heavy," she said. "Are you taking an art class or something?"

"Watercolor painting."

"Really? I didn't know you did that." She gave me another of those piercing looks. "How is it that we were best friends for three years and I never knew you were interested in art?"

"Because I never talked about it," I said. "It was like my dirty secret."

"Huh."

She seemed lost in thought as we made our way from Fairchilde Hall to the Memorial Union. We hadn't seen each other or spoken since the afternoon I'd found her and Barry together, screwing on our couch. That had been late last year, right before the end of spring term. It had been almost a whole year since I'd seen her.

Skylar was right. I had changed, and not just because my hair was longer. Living on my own on the mountain had changed me, made me more independent. Then Gage had come along, and that ... well, I wasn't sure what exactly it had done to me, just that I felt different inside.

Skylar, on the other hand, looked exactly the same. She still had her light brown hair dyed a brilliant red, still wore the cat-eye make-up she favored and the vintage fifties-style clothing. The only thing different about her was her apparent shame and regret over the Barry Incident.

I figured she ought to be ashamed. A true best friend keeps her mitts off her BFF's boyfriend, no matter how tempted she is.

We chatted about inconsequential stuff like the weather as we made our way up the huge marble staircase leading up to the mezzanine of the M.U. and took a table at the coffee shop there. It was almost like old times, except for the thin undercurrent of anxiety and resentment I could feel beneath our words. I guess the old times were gone forever.

We sat down with our lattes and I arranged my gear to be as out of the way as possible. Our little table gave us a great view of the upper hall of the M.U., which I always thought of as the promenade. That wasn't its real name, just how I thought of it. There was a double row of flags lining the hall, from almost every country in the world. Across the way, we could see a big slice of the M.U. lounge, which looked like a nineteen-twenties fantasy of a Medieval great hall.

A man strolled down the hall and took a seat on a bench situated almost directly across from our table. He wore a black suit, which seemed odd. Nobody wore suits on campus, except maybe in administration. Especially not formal-looking suits like that one. He caught me staring at him and smiled, but the smile didn't reach his eyes.

"So, you're not at Pioneer anymore?" Skylar said, jerking my attention away from the man in the suit.

"Nope," I said, toying uneasily with my hair. "I'm taking a few art classes and working at The Unique Boutique."

"Oh. Wow. What happened to pre-med?"

"It's not happening anymore. I decided I didn't want to be a doctor."

She blinked. "Huh. Okay. Wow, I'm just really surprised. I thought that was what you wanted more than anything."

"It was what my parents wanted more than anything," I said. "How about you? Still in the pharmacy program?"

"Yeah. I'm pretty much the same."

"Seeing anyone?"

She shook her head. "No. Are you?"

I glanced over at the bench. The man in the black suit was gone.

"Nova?"

"Huh?" I blinked at Skylar. "What were you saying?"

"I asked if you were seeing anyone."

"Nope." I took a sip of my latte. There was no way I was telling her about Gage. Even if she got me drunk, that story would never pass my lips.

She sighed, turning her paper coffee cup around and around in her hands. "Nova, I'm so sorry about what happened with Barry."

"Yeah, you already said that."

"I feel like you don't believe me."

I pursed my lips. "I'm not sure what you want me to say. I mean, you screwed my boyfriend."

"I'd like your forgiveness." She looked at me hopefully.

"I don't know if I'm ready for that," I said.

Skylar bent her head. I could see the line where her light-brown roots were starting to come in. "Okay. I guess I deserve that."

"I just don't think we can go back to where we were," I said. "I mean, what happens with the next guy? When I date someone else, are you going to go after him, too?"

"No." She looked up at me, her eyes wide and sincere. At least they looked sincere. I wasn't sure I could believe them.

"How do you know, Sky? I mean, you did Barry. Why did you do Barry, by the way?"

Her lip trembled. "I don't know," she said in a miserable tone. "I was lonely. I'd broken up with Pete. Remember Pete? I was feeling sorry for myself. Barry came over looking for you and you weren't there and we sat down on the couch to watch some TV and things kind of got out of hand."

"Yeah. Out of hand—that's one way to put it."

"I'll never do anything like that again," she said firmly.

I wanted to believe her. The problem was I knew how easy it was to say something like that. Following through was the hard part and Skylar had never been great at follow-through.

"You don't believe me, do you?"

Was I that transparent? I tilted my head, searching for the right words, ones that wouldn't hurt either of us too much and wouldn't be a complete lie.

"I want to," I said stiffly. "But I'm afraid."

"I guess I'll just have to prove myself," she said. Her gaze traveled across the coffee shop and out into the promenade. She brightened. "I have an idea. You've got more time now that you're not doing pre-med, right?"

"Yeah."

"We could go see a movie! That new Gage Dalton one is playing."

My face burned and my stomach gave a queasy flip. "My parents already took me to that one."

"Oh. Really? I thought they didn't do movies."

"It was kind of a special occasion. They were helping me move."

"Oh, I see. Did you like it? Was it any good? God, he's so hot. I'm totally in love with him."

I vaguely remembered her saying something to that effect back when we were roomies. "It was pretty good."

"Yeah? I heard there was a nude scene. Is it true? He's got the greatest body." She sighed dramatically. "He's my secret boyfriend, you know."

I swallowed hard. She didn't know my history with him and I couldn't blame her for prattling on about some guy who was really just a beautiful image and a fantasy to her. At the same time, I couldn't help bristling with secret jealousy and resentment when she talked that way. At least I hoped it was secret.

"I didn't feel well and I left early," I said. "I must have missed the nude scene."

"Oh. So you didn't really see it after all. You wanna go?"

"No." The word came out a lot more sharply than I'd meant it to. "Sorry. I'm just kind of tired and I don't like crime dramas that much anyway. Not my kind of thing."

"Oh." Her shoulders sagged. "Okay. Well, maybe some other time."

"Yeah. Some other time."

Chapter 5
Shadow Pattern

Nova:

My apartment building looked almost like a row of small condos or townhouses, all shoulder to shoulder with neatly trimmed shrubs in the front, each door with its own concrete path from the main sidewalk. No parking except on-street, of course, but otherwise respectable-looking and even kinda cute, especially on a sunny day, as long as you could ignore the mutant mushroom effect. That was the outside.

The insides weren't so nice. And even the exteriors, when you got close, didn't look so good. The only character the place had was all the wear and tear on it from decades of use and little maintenance. It certainly didn't have character designed in.

The bike ride back should have flushed all the frustration and resentment of Skylar out of my system, yet when I got home I still felt extremely tense. There seemed to be something dark lurking beneath the sparkling exterior of the day. The air felt almost heavy as I coasted up to my cheap and ugly front door.

Having seen Jeremy's ghost—he'd been the one to alert me that Gage needed help after falling in the river—I knew there really were unseen things in the world, existing side by side with us. However, I wasn't going to let that knowledge drive me nuts or make me paranoid. Whatever this feeling was, I wouldn't let it get to me. I would master it.

I glanced up and down the sidewalk, but it looked just as cheerful as it had moments before when I'd turned onto my street. Bare trees sent lacy shadow patterns across the bright pavement. A flock of chickadees fluttered around in the branches, cheeping at each other in happy voices. Everything looked beautiful.

Yet the creepy sensation remained. For some reason, the image of that man in the black suit popped into my head. He wasn't anywhere around, though. The street was empty of everything except sunshine.

Whatever it was had to be invisible. I could feel it but not see it. Or maybe it was just my kooky imagination, spitting up images from the horror movie phase I'd gone through in my teens. I'd never told my mom, but she'd been dead right about the horror movies. Bad idea. Apparently, I'm way too suggestible for scary stuff like that.

I stuck my key in the lock. In my peripheral vision, I saw movement. My head snapped around, but nothing was there except a naked red dogwood, its crimson twigs stark against a backdrop of dark-green juniper. Neither shrub so much as waved a branch in the still winter air.

Maybe a bird had flown by. Or it might have been a cat. Cats move quickly and don't make much noise.

Right. A cat.

I opened the door and went inside, locking myself in with a sigh of relief. Home safe. Winter sun streamed in through my none-too-clean living room window, making the apartment look almost as cheerful as the outdoors. The watercolor painting I'd started, based on one of the drawings I'd made of Gage, lit up in all the sun.

But I still couldn't shake that eerie feeling of being watched. This was the first time I wished I'd rented a nicer place. It's pretty standard for students to live in cheap, old apartments, but maybe a better place would have felt less creepy.

I had nothing but my mp3 player to take the edge off or change the atmosphere, and I didn't want to stick earbuds in my ears. That would cut me off from any noises that might warn me.

I had no idea what I'd need to be warned about. It was just the idea. Thinking that some creature or person could sneak up on me and I wouldn't hear it coming...well, that was worse than putting up with the ominous silence.

I did have my laptop. The sound on it was crappy, but better than nothing. I logged in to my streaming music service and let the sounds of Linkin Park's latest fill my living room.

That made me think of Gage and his guitar. Damn. Every time I thought I was getting over him, something would remind me of him and I'd be right back where I started. Take Skylar and her fangirl squeeing today.

For a second, I amused myself with a picture of her discovering I actually knew Gage personally. Oh, the lolz. Unfortunately, I had no photos of him and me together, no proof that I'd been with him.

Hah. I didn't want or need proof. I knew and that was what counted. I wouldn't go around blabbing about it anyway, even if I did have proof. It was just that moment of amusement I wanted, picturing Skylar's face.

The music seemed to banish the creepy feeling and I went into the kitchen to make myself a sandwich. I'd been living on peanut butter and canned soup lately.

I got out the bread and set a couple pieces on a paper towel. In the living room, the music cut off, interrupting Chevelle in the middle of the phrase "seeing red again."

I jumped. My heart jumped, too, and kept right on banging in a terrified sprint. The living room was utterly silent.

Had I lost my Internet connection? That could explain the music shutting off. No, I didn't have Wi-Fi here; I used a hard connection. It couldn't be that.

I inched my way across the tiny kitchen and peered around the dividing wall and into the living room. Empty, except for my floor pillows and the crate that supported my laptop. The tab on which I'd had the music channel was closed and all I could see was Instagram.

Wiring. It had to be the old wiring in this place. I stalked over to my laptop and removed the wall connection, leaving it on battery power.

The creepy, someone-is-watching-you sensation had disappeared. So to speak. The point is, I couldn't feel it anymore, so whatever had caused my music to shut off couldn't be supernatural. The creepiness had probably been only my wild imagination anyway.

All is well, Nova.

Right. All is well. I returned to the kitchen and my peanut butter sandwich, but for some reason I couldn't shake the image of Gage and his dead friend Jeremy.

***

A couple decades back, an artist had painted this pair of gigantic murals on the walls of the grand formal staircase in the Memorial Union. The bright colors and crisp design didn't really work for me. It seemed to fight with the vintage elegance of the rest of the design, especially with the cool gray marble of the steps themselves.

No-one had consulted me on the design, though. I hadn't even been talking in full sentences yet when it had been installed.

The domed ceiling rose overhead like an indoor sky. In the center of the dome hung an elaborate lantern with fancy metalwork. It cast equally fancy patterns of light and shadow across the ceiling and upper walls.

The Memorial Union was quickly becoming my favorite place to hang out because there were usually quite a few other people there. I needed crowds around me. If I couldn't get them on campus, I sometimes drove to the mall in Albany, the next town over, especially on weekends. The mall was almost always busy with shoppers trying to escape the rain.

The creepy just wasn't letting up. Since that first afternoon, I'd had several other instances of feeling watched. Part of me wanted to believe I was paranoid, because the alternative was believing I really was being watched. But by whom? And why?

It was getting hard to sleep. The only time I really felt safe was when I was around other people, like at work or on campus. Crowds were good. Being alone was not so good.

That was why I lingered on Friday after my art class. My shift at the boutique didn't start until five o'clock and I had plenty of time to kill, so I wanted to kill it with other people around.

I was dragging my portfolio up the echoing marble M.U. steps on my way to the coffee shop when two familiar figures caught my eye. Skylar, dressed like a weird mash-up of fifties church lady and pin-up girl. And guess whose arm she was hanging on? Yep. Barry.

He looked pretty much exactly the same as he had the last time I saw him. His light-brown hair was in the same short cut, he wore the same kind of workout gear over his lean frame, like he was always on his way to or from the gym. He was very attractive, in a boy next door kind of way. If that boy next door was a jock, anyhow.

And it didn't hurt me at all to see him, even with Skylar clinging to his arm. Weirdly, I felt almost nothing when I looked at him.

How strange to think I'd dated that guy. I'd actually thought I was in love with him, had accepted his offer of marriage. I'd freaked out and quit school over him and Skylar. Now, looking at them together, it almost felt like it had happened to someone else.

They were here and I was here. Perfect timing. Barry needed to know just how little I gave a damn about them being together. Maybe if I truly didn't care I wouldn't have bothered skewering them, but you know what they say about the taste of revenge and all that.

Sky turned almost as red as her hair when she saw I'd noticed them. Hah. Busted. I lifted my hand and gave an extra-cheery wave. Barry and Skylar exchanged an uncomfortable-looking glance.

"Hi, you guys!" I called out. I wasn't going to give them any quarter.

Skylar lifted an unenthusiastic hand in response to my greeting. Barry just stared at his Nike-clad feet.

I walked over to them. "I thought you weren't together."

Now it was Skylar's turn to stare at the floor. Barry shifted from one foot to the other, still trying to avoid my gaze.

"Hi, Nova," he said.

"Barry. You look exactly the same."

"You—uh—you look good."

Skylar lifted her head and glared at him. Her cat-eye makeup looked particularly harsh today in the unforgiving light of the M.U. steps.

"Thanks," I said. "Sky, you told me you weren't seeing Barry. What's up with that?"

"You told her that?" he said, glaring back at her. "Why would you do that?"

"I'm sorry." She squirmed. "I didn't know what else to say."

"The truth would have been good." Barry slipped her hand from his arm.

"Oops. I didn't mean to cause any trouble," I said. It was true, mostly. I didn't want to break them up, just make them uncomfortable.

"It's fine," Barry said between gritted teeth.

"Is it? You look kind of upset." I shifted my purse strap.

"That must make you real happy, Nova." He turned his glare on me.

"Actually, it doesn't." My voice sounded so cool and steady it surprised even me. "I don't give a damn who you see. I'm over you. Have fun together."

I hauled my gear past them and up the steps. I didn't know if they were watching me or if they continued down the way they'd been going when I'd first caught sight of them. Skylar had lied to me and I couldn't say I was all that surprised. It seemed to be a way of life for her.

Maybe she'd thought I would go after her if I knew she was with my ex. I scanned my inner landscape and found no trace of attachment to Barry. I was truly done with him, and that brought a smile to my face.

Mission accomplished, sort of. Barry clearly wasn't convinced I didn't care about him anymore. He'd figure it out eventually, though, when I continued to show no sign of giving a damn.

Now if I'd seen Skylar with Gage, I would have hurt her. Him, too. Barry, though, I couldn't have cared less what he did or with whom.

Maybe someday I'd feel the same way about Gage.

***

On the way to The Unique Boutique, I had to pass a little bookstore called Folkways Books. It had a narrow space in an early twentieth century stucco-covered brick building downtown, with a bay window display area and what looked like the original wooden door. I'd never been inside. It seemed to be the kind of place that carried a lot of odd-ball books, alternative spirituality and back to the land, DIY house building, find your inner Buddha titles. I didn't normally read that kind of stuff.

It had been there forever, as far as I knew. Since the seventies, anyway. It had a little of that hippie vibe still, with an unusual rotating collection of books in the old-fashioned window display case.

I'd wondered more than once if someone in there would understand about the creepy feelings I'd been having lately. Or maybe they had a book or two that would explain. So far, I hadn't had the nerve to find out.

Today, I went inside for the first time.

A string of tiny bells on the door tinkled when I entered. The overwhelming, sweetly exotic scent of incense met my nose inside, making the store seem foreign and almost otherworldly to my boring mainstream senses. I glanced around with no idea where to start looking.

The front desk, where the cashier stood, had a glass case full of Tarot decks and other stuff I couldn't identify. The front of the store held a small music section, and the rest of it was just rows of wooden bookshelves. Soft lighting suffused the whole place. Here and there a potted plant brightened up a shelf.

There was nothing scary about it at all. Counter-cultural, maybe, but not spooky the way I'd half expected. It had a gentle, almost playful air.

I wandered back, glancing at the spines. They didn't look like esoteric tomes, being brightly colored and glossy trade paperbacks. I'd always pictured books about ghosts and the paranormal to be ancient, leather-bound objects, not ordinary modern books. Some of them sounded interesting—auras, chakras, dream interpretation. Others were just weird. Bigfoot? Really? Alien abduction? I couldn't get my head around those.

Apparently, though, some people took that stuff seriously.

I was staring at a book that purported to teach astral projection, wondering if it could possibly work, when a small dark-haired woman walked up to me. She wore ordinary-looking jeans and a plain blue jean jacket, with her long hair streaked with silver and tied back in a ponytail. I would have assumed she was there to peruse the astral-projection books, except for the way she was looking so directly at me.

I looked back, a little apprehensively.

She smiled, her eyes crinkling at the corners. "Hi. I know this is going to sound weird, but I'm getting the feeling you have some questions I might be able to answer."

"Uh..." Was it that obvious that I needed help? I wasn't comfortable accepting it from a total stranger who took it upon herself to approach me, though.

"I have a lot of experience with all this." She gestured at the books.

"Astral projection?"

"Psychic matters. Spirits." She stuck out her hand. "I'm Marie. I don't usually come up to strangers like this, but you look kind of lost."

"Yeah, I guess I am." I shook her hand. It was slightly calloused and warm, strong for her small size.

"I'm not trying to pressure you or anything," she said with a shrug. "If you don't want to talk, that's okay."

"No. I—uh—I do need some help."

She cocked her head. "Okay. What's going on?"

I glanced around the store. We were alone on this aisle, thank goodness, because I really didn't want anyone else listening in on the conversation. It was too bizarre. Part of me felt like an idiot even talking about spirits at all, even though I'd come in here driven by the need to find some answers.

"I feel like I'm being watched," I said finally. My face flushed. "That sounds totally paranoid, I know. But there's never anyone there, yet I feel like someone is staring at me."

"Hmm," Marie said. "Do you feel it now?"

"No. It's usually strongest when I'm alone."

"It could be a spirit of some kind. Do you mind if I do a short reading?"

My brows crimped. "Reading?"

"Yeah. Of your energy. Your aura, if you will." She smiled again, her eyes warm. "Don't worry, it doesn't hurt."

I let out a nervous chuckle. She seemed harmless, and she was only going to look at me, so it should be fine. "Okay. Sure, why not?"

Her eyes lost their focus as she looked at me. It was like she was gazing not at me but at the air around me. No, that's not right. I can't quite describe what it looked like because I'd never seen anything like it before. She was seeing something that was invisible to me.

"There's something dark attached to you," she said, her voice soft and low. "Dangerous. I can't see exactly what it is. It's hiding its true nature from me."

Icy fingers seemed to walk their way up my spine. This wasn't fun anymore. "You're scaring me."

Marie blinked and her eyes resumed their normal focus. "I'm sorry. I didn't mean to scare you."

I crossed my arms over my chest. "It's okay. I'm fine."

"No." She rested her hand briefly on my forearm. "I was too intense. I should have been more careful."

"You really think this thing is dangerous?"

Her brow wrinkled and her mouth flattened. "It's hard to say for sure. I need to know more about the entity before I can give you details. But I'd be careful if I were you."

I glanced around again, suddenly even more nervous, as if the thing or entity might be sneaking up on me from behind. "How? I have no idea how to fight this thing."

"Do you believe in any kind of higher power?"

"You mean like God?"

"God, Goddess, yes. A benevolent power in the universe. Ask that power to watch over you. For now, that's all I can tell you." She glanced around us, kind of the same way I had. "This store is great, but it's not the best place to have a conversation like this."

"Yeah. I guess not."

"Look, if you want to talk more, I'll give you my number. You can call me anytime." She reached into the plain, black leather purse she carried, looking at me inquiringly as she did.

"Uh ... sure. Yeah, that would be good." I figured it couldn't hurt. She didn't seem to be running a scam, asking me for money or anything like that.

She pulled out a scrap of paper and a pen, scribbled something, handed the scrap to me. "I'm serious, now. Anytime. Don't worry about bothering me. What's your name, by the way?"

"Nova."

She grinned at me. "Nova. I like it. Give me a call and we'll talk."

Chapter 6
Watched

As I biked across the quad early Saturday morning, I could feel someone watching me. The quad is a big square, kind of like a combination park and town square, between the M.U. and Milton, one of the really big lecture halls. It's mostly grass lawn and concrete sidewalks, with a couple of enormous sequoia trees and some flowering plums and cherries, bare in January, and smaller shrubs.

On weekdays, it's full of students going to and from classes or heading to the M.U. to hang out and study. At five thirty on a Saturday, it's usually completely empty. Dark, too, at this time of year. Fog clung to the skirts of the sequoias and hid the rhododendron and azalea banks from me, making them look like old furniture covered in drop cloths in some forgotten and haunted mansion.

Someone was following me. I assumed it was the same someone I'd sensed that other day, when my laptop had freaked out. He—it—had given up merely watching and was actively following me now.

I had no evidence for this assertion, just my intuition. A hunch, plus the fact that, at this very moment, I could feel eyes on me as I biked across the quad before dawn.

Maybe he thought he could intimidate me, force me to hide out in my apartment. Well, that wasn't going to happen. He couldn't stop me from living my life. Unfortunately, making me constantly wonder what was happening to me was well within his capabilities.

I had a painting I wanted to work on in the studio because it was a still life and we were supposed to paint from the arrangement the professor had made. I had a shift at the boutique later today, so I'd come in early to get the studio work done. It was a week after I'd bumped into Skylar.

To all appearances, I was the only person on the quad at this hour.

I looked around as my bike glided into the center of the quad. No-one to be seen, although I supposed a perv could be hiding in the banks of rhodies or maybe under one of the giant sequoias on the other side of the huge open space. But why?

Yeah, occasionally female students were attacked on campus. Even male students sometimes had violent encounters. But this wasn't completely random; this was purposeful and aimed at me in particular. Why me?

I was no-one special. Why would anyone follow me, try to scare me? It didn't make sense to me.

On Thursday, I'd felt it when I'd left the boutique on my lunch break, and then again when I'd gone home. The sense of being watched had actually followed me all the way back to my apartment, although I couldn't identify anyone trailing me.

I was paranoid. That was the only explanation for it. Either that or I was being stalked, and I couldn't think of anyone who would bother stalking somebody like me.

The press? Nah. Why would they care? Gage's disappearance was months ago and his PR people had already explained it well enough to satisfy the public.

I supposed it could be someone in one of my two classes or someone who'd come into the boutique. Maybe some random stranger had fixated on me for reasons I couldn't even guess. Whoever it was, and whatever their reasons, it was making me jumpy and irritable and I hated it.

I skirted Fairchilde Hall and locked up my bike on the rack behind the building. The parking lot was nearly empty at this time, with only one car plus my bike. I glanced around nervously, but saw no-one. Just the row of shrubs at the edge of the lot, bathed in a sickly orange glow from the sodium lights, the intramural field beyond the shrubs, and in the distance the security lights of Sackett Hall, one of the dorms.

Not a person in sight.

I went into the art building and shut the door behind me. They normally left it open for students like me who wanted to work on projects at odd hours. But I locked it. Just so no-one could come in behind me and surprise me.

The feeling was weaker inside the building, but I still couldn't shake it. Even the familiar, comforting smells of linseed oil and turpentine, the reassuring sight of canvases and watercolor paper, the artful tumble of the still life the prof had arranged couldn't settle my nerves. As I set up my work space, I kept glancing behind myself, half expecting to find some creepy pervert standing there. Except, of course, no-one was.

At one point, I stopped to take a quick break. I walked across the studio and the gray-walled gallery in the front room to the long, Victorian-style windows that marked Fairchilde Hall as the former nineteenth-century mansion it was, and looked outside. I don't know why I looked. It was just a random sort of glance, but I saw him.

Pale early morning sunlight illuminated a blond guy standing on the sidewalk beneath the huge spruce tree in front of the building. My whole body gave a jolt of shock at the sight of him. He looked just the same. I remembered him well, even after all those months.

He was wearing the same flannel shirt and jeans. Looking straight at me. He could see me; I was sure of it. What did he want? Why was he here?

I dashed for the front door. Outside, no-one stood beneath the spruce tree. The leafless azalea shrubs, their buds fat with coming blooms, could not have hidden a grown man. Jeremy was gone.

Shivering, I went back inside the building. Why would Jeremy come here? Was he trying to warn me of something? Was Gage in trouble? The only time I'd seen him before was when Gage had fallen in the river, and that worried me.

If he was in trouble, if he'd gotten hurt, I wouldn't find out about it until much later, after it had hit the media. I was no-one special in his life, even if it had felt that way for a short time. No-one would bother informing me.

My worries made focusing on my painting difficult.

Two hours later, I was starving because I hadn't eaten breakfast. The painting was far from finished, but I could stop and take a break. Besides, it's important in watercolor to let your work dry between washes or successive layers of paint, something I had a hard time doing. I needed to learn patience, and besides I was tired of the prof telling me I was pulling up the underlying layers of paint and making mud on my paper.

I washed my brushes and my hands, put away all my supplies and left my piece to dry flat. Fairchilde Hall was right across the street from the M.U., which had a few restaurants open even on Saturdays. I'd go there and pick up something quick.

As I gathered my jacket and purse, that sense of something watching me returned, hard and heavy. It was so strong, it almost felt physical, like some unseen creature was breathing on the back of my neck. I shivered and headed out of the studio and through the student gallery in the front room, eager to get somewhere with other people.

They were running an art show of some kind, featuring figure drawings, mostly in pastel. I paused next to one of a voluptuous woman, her curves rendered in flowing red and purple lines.

"Nova." The whisper was deep and masculine, but not a voice I recognized.

I whirled around, heart pounding. The gallery was empty of everything except me and the collection of life drawings on the dull gray walls. I was alone and letting my imagination run away with me. Big time.

I turned for the front door.

"Nova." Louder this time.

I whirled again. Still alone. Sweat bloomed all over me.

"What?" I snapped. "Who are you? Quit fucking with me."

He laughed.

That just pissed me off. What kind of perv—no, sorry, that's not fair to all the kind and considerate pervs in the world. What kind of flaming asshole follows a woman around, whispering at her, while she's alone? And won't even show his face?

"I can tell you think you're funny," I said. "I don't."

I took another couple of strides toward the door. The old floorboards squeaked beneath my feet. Something grabbed me. Whatever it was spun me around and shoved me toward the nearest wall. I still couldn't see him.

Light from the windows filled the room, yet I couldn't see my assailant. He was invisible. I shrieked in startled terror as hard invisible hands pressed me against the plaster. My shoulder bumped against one of the drawings, knocking it off-kilter, its black and ocher swirling in my peripheral vision.

He—it—growled. I mean growled, like a huge dog or maybe a mountain lion. A predator. I could hear the sound vibrating in its throat, even though I couldn't see the throat.

Throwing up my arms, I tried to pry the thing off me. My arms met no resistance, yet the creature didn't budge. I mean, I couldn't feel its arms. Its hands or paws or whatever still shoved me against the wall and it continued to growl ferociously. But I couldn't feel any other part of its body.

God. What was going on here? What was this thing?

"Tell Gage," the creature said in an even deeper voice than before, the register so low it barely sounded human. "Tell Gage."

"W-what?"

"Tell him."

A door banged somewhere else in the building. The creature let go of me. The pressure on my shoulders ceased and the voice went silent. I stood there, trembling all over, listening to the new arrival's footfalls on the old wooden floorboards.

Slowly my hands rose again, feeling for whatever had been attacking me, but just as before, I couldn't feel anything. It seemed to be gone.

The new person didn't come into the gallery. I could hear footsteps moving toward the offices at the other end of the building, so it was probably a staff member. My hand rose to push back my hair, and it shook so badly I almost stuck myself in the eye.

Holy hell. I'd been attacked by—by what? A demon? A ghost?

I tottered to the front door. My whole body trembled. I needed to run, to work off the adrenaline.

Maybe I'm crazy.

The thought of possible insanity actually comforted me for approximately five seconds. Because madness seemed less scary than whatever that thing was, assuming it was real. But I didn't think I was truly insane.

Didn't insane people automatically think their delusions were real? Didn't the fact that I questioned my experience mean I wasn't completely out of touch with reality? I didn't know how true that was, but it sounded reasonable and I was going with it.

My stomach growled almost as fiercely as the monster had. I still had an appetite, even after demon attack.

The M.U. had fewer people in it than on weekdays, but there were enough so I didn't feel as terrified as when I was alone. And these people seemed happy. It was Saturday, after all, and presumably none of them had just been attacked by an invisible monster. I ran up to the coffee shop on the promenade, got myself a huge latte and a giant scone, and soaked up the happy-normal energy.

It wasn't enough.

I could swear someone was still watching me. *He* was still watching me. It would be easy for him to do, after all, since he was invisible. I'm sure that opened up a whole lot of possibilities for him.

What if I was wrong about him not attacking me here? What if he didn't care who saw? Except he'd stopped as soon as another person had entered the art building, so it seemed like a reasonable assumption.

Maybe nothing would be enough to put me fully at ease, at least for a while. How did you recover from something like that? I wanted to scrub myself head to toe, inside and out. I wanted to run into a church and hide behind the altar, even though I had no idea whether that would do any good.

Maybe I'd go to church tomorrow. It had been a long while, but I suddenly had some motivation.

Crap. I was going to have to go home at some point, and that was the last thing I wanted. To be alone in my apartment, vulnerable to that thing again? Ick. No way. But I couldn't stay out forever. The M.U. would close for the night, so unless I was prepared to wander the streets until dawn, I had to go home.

Maybe I couldn't stay out forever, but that didn't mean I couldn't put off going home as long as possible. Like all day and part of the night. Hah. Take that, invisible monster.

Tell Gage.

The creature's words came back to me in a startling rush. It had something to do with Gage, otherwise why would it have said that?

Holy hell. Maybe *this* was his awful secret. I had no real idea what *this* was, except it clearly had a supernatural element. An evil one.

And Gage had believed he was protecting me by not telling me the details. Well, that was obviously not true. What would that thing do the second time it came after me?

I could think of all kinds of possibilities, each more gruesome than the last.

If only I had Gage's number. I'd made no attempt to get it, considering how hard he'd tried to get away from me. If he didn't want me, I sure wasn't going after him. But things had changed and I wanted answers. ASAP.

To his handlers, I'd probably be nothing more than another fan if I tried to get through to him, though. Even Cindy, who might remember my name. She obviously hadn't liked me, so I couldn't count on help from that quarter.

At the moment, there wasn't much to do except avoid going home. And the movie theater. I didn't relish the thought of sitting in a dark room, even one filled with tons of other people.

In the end, I hung around the M.U., making sketches, people watching. I headed up to the lounge to watch some TV for half an hour, then stopped by the store for a couple of paperback novels. There were plenty of nooks and crannies in the M.U. for someone like me to curl up and read. All in all, a pleasant Saturday, except for the ominous cloud that seemed to hang over me the whole time.

Eventually, the M.U. closed down for the night. Gack. Now I had to ride my bike home. Let myself into my empty apartment.

My stomach churned uneasily as I unlocked my bike and started back toward the apartment. The sun had gone down a couple of hours before, so it was dark except for streetlights. People still drove and walked around, though. Not too bad. Yet.

How was I going to sleep knowing that thing could come back at any time? Should I go back to Portland, move in with my parents?

No. Then I'd only bring it down on my family. I had to find some way to fight against it.

Chapter 7

A Twist In My Belly

Gage:

You ever had one of those dreams where you're just watching the action from the outside, and nothing you do or say makes any difference at all to the outcome?

Yeah. They suck.

In this one, I could see Nova. I could even feel her fear, feel her heart slamming inside her ribcage, feel heavy hands on her shoulders, pushing her against the wall. I could see the creature looming over her, like black mist in a vaguely humanoid shape. But larger. Much larger. The thing had horns and a tail. It looked just like one of those old-time demons or maybe something out of my own hometown.

Only this wasn't Hollywood.

Nova screamed. Her voice felt like a knife slicing through my innards.

I woke up with a gasp, already sitting upright, staring around the darkness of my bedroom without really seeing it. The darkness hid the emptiness of my room from me. All my eyes could take in was a wall of dark. It looked just like the blackness in my dream.

Dream. It was just a dream. But it felt so damned real, like I was connected to her soul and could see what was happening to her.

I staggered out of bed, sweating, heart pounding ferociously. The floor felt cold and hard beneath my bare feet. I dragged my fingers through my hair, trying to order my thoughts.

Phone. I had to find my phone and call Nova. Make sure she was okay.

I'd sworn I'd stay away from her, but things had changed. If she was hurt...if *he* had done something to her...

I snagged my jeans off the floor and fished my phone from the back pocket. Hit speed dial on the number she'd given me. I'd entered it the day I'd left her, but never used it until now.

The phone rang and rang and rang.

"Come on," I muttered under my breath. "Nova, pick up. Come on, pick up."

I'm sorry. The number you have reached is not in service. Please hang up and dial again.

I'm sorry. The number you have reached is not in service. Please hang up and dial again.

I nearly threw the goddamn thing at the wall. She'd given me her number, but apparently had changed it. Maybe she didn't want to hear from me. Maybe she wanted me to leave her alone.

I couldn't blame her, especially after I'd left the way I had.

I had Cindy on speed-dial too. I hit her number, tapping my bare foot on the floor in impatience as I waited for her to answer.

My bedroom window looked out over a canyon. I couldn't see the sunrise because it faced west, but I could see the sky gradually lightening. Dawn was on its way. Gray light crept into my even grayer bedroom. The world was waking up, so where the fuck was Cindy?

"Um...hello?" she said, her voice fuzzy and half-asleep.

"Cindy. It's me."

"Gage? What—why are you calling me at—do you know what time it is?"

"Yeah." I tapped my fingers against my bare leg. "It's six o'clock. Time to get up."

"Jesus." She groaned. "I never get up before eight. You know that."

"I need you to find someone for me."

"What? Who?"

"Nova Pennyman. The number I have for her is out of service. Hire a detective if you have to, but I want a good number for her by this afternoon."

She gave a pained sigh. "You want me to find that redneck chick?"

"She's not a redneck, for chrissake. And even if she was, I don't care. Just find her."

"Gage, what is going on?" She sounded fully awake now.

"Nothing. I just want to talk to her." I couldn't tell Cindy I'd had a bad dream. She'd never understand.

"Couldn't it have waited until later? In fact, can't you just look her up on Facebook or Tumblr?"

"No. I need to get hold of her now, not wait for her to friend me."

I would go to Avery's Crossing, on the chance she'd returned there after the cabin. If she wasn't there, at least I'd be in Oregon and I could follow her trail.

Another pained sigh. "All right. I'll have it to you by, say, three o'clock?"

"Sooner if you can. Cancel my appointment with the shrink and get me on a flight to Avery's Crossing. Drop everything else. I'm serious."

"Jesus," Cindy said. "All right, fine. Drop everything, get you to Oregon, find Nova Pennyman."

"That's my girl."

She hung up, muttering.

I wasn't going back to sleep, so I took myself downstairs and made some instant coffee. It was crap, but better than nothing. I needed to be alert for whatever was coming next.

My attempts to free myself from The Deal had come to nothing so far. Nobody seemed to know a thing, not even the people at the occult shops. And I hadn't mentioned it to my shrink, who would have had me on some kind of dire medication if he'd even suspected I thought I was being persecuted by the devil. We'd talked about Jeremy and my using, but I'd left out the supernatural shit.

So far I'd failed to figure out how to free myself. And now Nova might be in imminent danger because of me. I didn't know how to fight the devil, but I was going to learn. If necessary, I'd put myself in front of her. Offer myself to him. There was no way I'd let him take Nova.

***

Nova:

My neighborhood, which usually seemed so safe in the middle of the day, now looked like the set of a horror movie. The kind that's set in suburbia, where the houses are built on an old graveyard or something. You know—totally normal except for the evil that lurks beneath the perfectly manicured lawns.

The houses seemed to watch me as I biked along my street, their eyes blank and dark. Even the parked cars seemed to have some sort of primitive consciousness. Everything seemed darker than it should be, the orange halos of light from the streetlights leaving most of the neighborhood unlit and unsee-able.

No other humans livened the place. I was alone.

I coasted onto the sidewalk in front of my unit. The pool of light from the streetlight gave up just before it reached my front stoop, leaving it in black shadow. My wonderful landlord had failed, once again, to replace the bulb in my security light, so my front door looked like the black hole from hell.

Oh, God. That little private joke wasn't so funny anymore.

In the darkness, an even darker shadow stood waiting. I stopped dead, my heart pounding frantically again. Someone lurked there at my front door. A big someone. Had the watcher taken physical form now? My stomach turned so hard I thought for an instant I would throw up.

The guy had a baseball cap on, pulled low so I couldn't see much of his face, plus a loose, dark-blue canvas jacket and baggy jeans. He carried a large guitar case. There was something oddly familiar about him, although I couldn't place him. I stood there astride my bike, staring, afraid to go forward. Not sure how to handle whatever was about to happen.

I had a bike. He was on foot. I could get away—unless he was a demon, anyway.

"Are—what are you doing here?" I said, trying to keep my voice from shaking.

"I would have called but your number is different."

My mouth went even drier than it already was. "Gage?" I whispered.

Good God, of all the things that could have happened that day...after being attacked in the art building...I could hardly believe he was real. Why today?

He walked out of the shadows and into the light cast by the nearest street lamp. "I didn't mean to scare you."

He seemed even taller than I remembered. The baggy clothes hid the athletic shape of his body, yet I could still see the lines of him beneath the disguise. Even the cap and the scruffy beard couldn't hide his identity from me now that I'd realized who he was.

His blue eyes seemed dark and mysterious in the harsh lighting, but the chiseled planes of his cheekbones, the sharp straight nose—it was Gage.

My whole body contracted in longing. He was so close, yet I couldn't touch him while he remained just out of reach. Had I said I was over him? What a joke. I'd never be over him.

I couldn't stop staring. "What are you doing here?"

"Do you want me to go?"

"No!" I took a breath. "No, I didn't mean it that way. It's just that you surprised me."

My hands were shaking again. I was a nervous wreck today.

"I have to talk to you," he said, his voice so even it sounded like he was making an effort to keep it that way. "Can I come in for a while?"

"Of course. You didn't even have to ask." I got my keys out of my pocket and dismounted my bike, hoping he couldn't tell how trembly I was. "How did you find me, though?"

"Cindy hired someone to do a search. Then I flew in, came right over but you weren't here. I didn't want to miss you, so I just sat down and waited."

"Oh, my God." I stuck the key in the lock and gave him a sidelong glance. I liked the beard. It gave him a raffish, sexy look, but was short enough I could still see the hard, definite line of his jaw. "How long have you been here?"

"I don't know. A few hours."

"I've been out. I'm sorry. If I'd known you were here, I would've come straight home."

"Not your fault." He shrugged. "I called your new number, but I kept getting sent to voicemail."

"Weird. I must have turned off my phone."

I opened the door, wheeled my bike inside, waited for him to follow me. God, my apartment. It was even more embarrassing than the cabin had been. At least the cabin had charm. This place was just old and worn out. And it smelled funny.

He wasn't looking at the bare spots and stains in the carpet, the smudges on the dirty beige walls, or at my almost complete lack of furniture, though. He was looking at me. I couldn't read the expression in his eyes. Hope? Sorrow? Hesitation, maybe. Yeah, there was a lot of hesitation.

"I'm glad to see you," I said, wishing I could throw my arms around him and fuse my mouth to his. At the same time, anger began to stir. He hadn't called me in all those weeks. Would it have been so difficult to look me up a month ago?

It was unreal having him in my place again after I'd thought I'd never see him. I couldn't stop looking at him. Gage was here, with me. My body ached to feel him against me, yet I had the bewildering urge to slap him.

He set down the guitar case, propping it against the wall by the door. Then he took off the cap and stuck it in his jacket pocket. "I'm sorry I didn't get in touch sooner. I thought I was protecting you," he said with a grimace.

I folded my arms across my chest. "Were you? I mean, I know you said that, but you could have called."

He sighed. "I was afraid I'd endanger you."

For a minute, I just stared at him. He seemed sincere, but he was an actor after all. I didn't want to give up my indignation. I had a right to be upset, and to an explanation. Yet I didn't want to fight with him.

"You hurt me." My throat hurt right now.

He looked at the floor. "I know."

"You couldn't even leave a message or text me?"

"I told you. I was protecting you."

I shook my head. "I still don't understand why talking to me is so dangerous."

"I know, and I'm going to explain everything."

"You promise?"

He pressed a hand to his chest. "I swear it."

"Because if you don't, if you just lead me on and leave again, I don't want you to come back. I'm not the kind of girl who's willing to take that from a guy."

He met my eyes squarely, his gaze both calm and sincere. "You'll know everything before you go to bed tonight."

"Okay then." I glanced around my pitiful interior. "Do you want something to drink? To eat? I haven't got much, but I can get you a peanut-butter sandwich."

"How about we order in? I have a lot to tell you."

I stared at him a moment longer. "Okay. Um. Me too. I have a lot to tell you too." Like that an invisible something had attacked me and asked for him specifically. That ought to get his attention.

We ordered Indian food. Waiting for it felt awkward. There was this gulf between us, and it almost felt like I didn't know him anymore. I guess that isn't so strange, since we'd only spent eight days together, but it disappointed me.

I got us a couple of beers and we sat down at my rickety thrift-store table to wait for the food. He was so close to me. I could have reached across the table and touched his hand, but I didn't. Instead I just sat there, fiddling with my beer while my stomach did back-flips inside my belly.

Gage lifted his beer and glanced at me. "How have you been, Nova?"

"Oh, fine." Not fine. Not at all.

"I missed you like hell."

I stared again. I was doing a lot of that tonight. "Really?"

He nodded, sipping the beer. "Really."

"Oh. Wow. I missed you too."

He smiled. "Really?"

"Like crazy. I saw that movie you were in and I couldn't stand it. I had to leave early."

His smile disappeared. "God, I'm sorry. I shouldn't have left you like that."

"I understood," I said with a shrug. "You had to go back. You had people depending on you."

He gestured with the beer bottle. "Yeah, but it didn't have to be like that. I was an ass."

I took a swig of my own beer, trying desperately to cover up my nervousness. "I'm glad you came to see me."

He looked around the open-plan kitchen and living room combo. "Do you have a couch?"

"Nope. I haven't gotten around to buying one yet. I do have a couple of big pillows, though."

"Let's sit on the floor together."

We took our beers over to the giant corduroy pillows I'd bought for the place and sank to the old, brown carpet. At least I'd vacuumed yesterday. The light from the cheap brass chandelier over the dinette table cast ugly bars of shadow over the living room.

Gage looked over at me. He put his arm around my shoulders. "Is this okay?"

"I've been waiting for you to do that."

He drew me up against his hard, hot body. God, that felt good. I put my arm across his hard, narrow waist and nestled my head against his chest. He smelled faintly of soap and healthy male skin, a hint of sweat. I remembered that smell, and so did my body. It made my core contract again in longing.

"Did you ever find out what happened to your wallet?" I said.

He'd lost his wallet some time after leaving a house party and falling in the McKenzie River, where I'd later found him and pulled him out. He'd actually accused me of stealing it—one of several things we'd squabbled over when we first met. Eventually, though, we'd settled our differences.

"No, I never did," he said. "I'm pretty sure someone at the party lifted it."

"I'm sorry about that."

"I'm over it." He rested his cheek on the top of my head. "I missed you so damn much."

"We really haven't known each other very long." Now why had I reminded him of that?

"I know. But it doesn't seem to matter."

"No, it doesn't." I tipped my face up. "I can hardly believe you're here. I'm not dreaming, am I?"

He smiled that incredible smile of his. "No. Unless I'm dreaming too."

Abruptly, a shadow settled over his face. Not just a frown, but a darkening of his whole expression.

"Gage?" I said.

His lips flattened. "I had a nightmare about you. Some really fucked up shit."

I felt an odd little twist in my belly. It couldn't be coincidence, not after what had happened to me in Fairchilde. "When?"

"This morning. It's why I came." He shook his head with a rueful twist of his beautiful mouth. "I sound crazy, huh? I just had to make sure you're okay."

Chapter 8

Confession

Nova:

Gage must have cared about me, or he wouldn't have bothered coming so far just because of a bad dream. Or maybe he only felt he owed me. I couldn't forget the way I'd blurted out that I loved him, right before he'd gotten on the helicopter, and I wasn't going to say it again until I had a better idea of how he felt in return. Besides, even with him here, I wasn't sure it was true. How could I love someone I'd only known for a week?

"You look great," he said, gazing down at me, his arm still around me. "Was I worrying over nothing?"

"Well, I'm still in one piece," I said, thinking of the art gallery incident.

His frown turned to an outright scowl. "One piece? What does that mean?"

He wasn't going to like hearing about this, but he ought to know, especially since he'd come to see me.

I looked up into his concerned gaze. "Something really weird happened to me this morning."

I described the events in the art building for him. As I spoke, his face became more and more grim and angry. I couldn't tell if he was angry with me or someone else, although I had no idea why he'd blame me. It's not like I could have protected myself against something I never would have guessed was even possible before it happened.

I drew away from his embrace. "You look like you want to break something."

"I do. God damn it." He shook his head, his square jaw clenching. "I should have known it wasn't enough."

"What wasn't enough? What's going on, anyway?"

He didn't respond. He just stared down at his lap, his arm hanging at his side. It seemed pretty obvious he didn't want to answer.

"Gage?"

He gave me an embarrassed-looking glance. "Remember at the cabin when I told you I was involved in something dangerous?"

"Yeah. You wouldn't tell me what it was." I'd wondered at the time if it had something to do with the drug trade.

"I—uh—" He closed his eyes, shaking his head again. "Christ. I've never told anyone this and it's really hard to say."

"I promise not to laugh."

He opened one eye. "You don't know what you're saying."

"So tell me."

An enormous sigh escaped him. "Shit. Okay." He took a deep breath. "When I was ten, my mom made a deal with the devil."

I blinked. Had I heard that correctly? I squinted at him and blinked again. "The devil. You mean, like the Devil-devil?"

"Is there some other devil?"

"How the hell would I know?" I put my hand over my mouth. "I didn't mean to say that."

His mouth curved, but it wasn't a real smile. "Yes, it was the devil-devil. The real thing. She traded my soul for success in the movie business."

Now I really stared, my mouth open. "What? She—hold on. She traded *your* soul? What kind of deal is that? What kind of mom does that?"

"The kind more interested in her kid making it big in the movies than in raising him," he said calmly.

"I can't—I just can't—" I stopped and stared again. "Are you for real? You're not pranking me?"

"I'm so not pranking you. I'd never make up something like this."

"Holy...God." I shook my head. "I don't have words. I didn't even think people did that, like for real. It sounds like something out of a low-budget horror flick."

"I know, right?" He laughed a little. "I guess you can't fault her for lack of imagination."

"I can. I can fault her for a lot of things." His mom had officially pissed me off, forever, until the end of time. She didn't deserve a son like Gage. She didn't deserve a kid at all.

Moms are supposed to love their kids, protect them, teach them how to live. Not barter them like they're choice cuts of meat. I wanted to tell that awful woman exactly what I thought of her and I would have if she'd been there.

"So you don't hate me?" he said.

I had to blink again. "Why would I hate you?"

"I brought that thing down on you. I drew its attention to you."

I didn't want to give him a glib answer, so I thought about it for a second. I certainly didn't hate him. Was I mad at him? He'd tried to protect me in the only way he knew how, and it wasn't his fault that I'd been the one to pull him from the river. I couldn't see how blaming him would make any sense.

Besides, it wasn't anger I felt at the moment. It was more like concern, love—er, strong affection—fury at his mom, worry about his safety...not hate.

"No," I said. "I sure don't hate you and I'm not mad at you. Only at your mom. She was supposed to take care of you, not trade you."

He hugged me, bending his head down to press a kiss to the top of my head. I wanted more.

"Thank you, baby," he said.

"I probably wouldn't have believed you if I hadn't had that thing happen today," I said. "I'd think you were exaggerating or something. Do you think it was the devil who grabbed me?"

"I don't know," he said, his eyes troubled again. "Maybe it was some lesser demon. But I'm sure it was because of The Deal, especially since the thing mentioned me."

I could hear the capital letters when he said "The Deal." It reminded me of all those talks we'd had at the cabin, about his career, my school.

"Is that why you think you didn't earn your success?" I said.

"Yeah. Because I didn't."

"But, Gage, you're really good. I don't think you should beat yourself up about what your mom did. It's not your fault, and you're a great actor in spite of her cheating."

He just stared down at me, a half smile on his lips.

"What?" I said.

"You really believe that?"

"Yes. I wouldn't say it if I didn't believe it."

"Did you know there was a joke going around on the Internet for a while that I'd made a deal with the devil for my fame? It's still knocking around if you look for it."

I snorted. "That's bullshit. You've got an Academy Award, for crying out loud. People are just jealous. They can't stand that someone else is famous or successful when they're not."

"Yeah, except it's true."

"No, it's not. Your mom made the deal. Not you."

He stared at me for another minute. His free hand came up to caress the side of my face. "I never thought that made a difference."

"It does to me."

His thumb brushed along the edge of my cheekbone. "I've always thought of myself as a fraud."

"No." I laid my hand over his. "You're not a fraud. Don't ever think that about yourself."

He still looked deeply troubled, with lines between his eyebrows and at the corners of his eyes, his lips tense. "He said he'd take me at the height of my fame. And that if for some reason he couldn't get me, he'd take all the people I cared about."

I tried to digest that. "Do you think he was trying to take me?"

"God, I hope not." He scowled. "My mom is convinced he made Jeremy overdose, though."

I felt my eyes widen. "Do you believe her?"

"I don't know. I've always laughed off her fears about him, but when I found Jeremy's body, something was there in the room with me. Something invisible. I've felt it other places since then, like it's following me around. That's why I was so worried about protecting you. But then I had that dream and I thought—" He swallowed hard, his gaze drawing away as he stared at my blank apartment wall. "I thought he might have come after you, and if I couldn't protect you by staying away then maybe we should be together after all."

Blue eyes slid quickly to mine, then away.

"If you want to, that is," he added.

"I want to."

"I wouldn't blame you if you didn't," he said, talking right over me. "I mean, I've brought all this shit into your life, gotten you attacked and everything. And it might not stop here. He might come after you again. What if it gets worse? And even without the supernatural crap, there's the fame, the lack of privacy, the—"

"Gage." I nudged him with my elbow.

"Huh?" He stopped talking to look down at me.

"I want to be with you."

He gazed at me a moment longer. Then his mouth came down on mine, fiercely sensual, hot and wet, and within seconds I was moaning. My arms went around his neck as his hand cupped my face.

In that moment, it was as if we hadn't been parted at all. Our bodies remembered each other, remembered exactly what to do. He licked me and I opened for him and he moaned as he plunged into me.

God, that sound turned me on.

I turned without breaking the kiss and climbed on his lap, straddling him, one knee on either side of his hips. His hands slid down my back and then up under the shirt I wore, spanning me, hot against my skin. I took his face in my hands, as if he might try to get away from me, and devoured his mouth.

His lips—God, his lips. The lower one, so full and bite-able. I'd missed the sensation of his mouth on mine so much over these last weeks. I took that lower lip between my teeth and pulled.

He dragged me closer, crushing my aching core against the bulge inside his jeans, making me whimper with pleasure. His hands cupped my ass, fingers curving around my cheeks, squeezing. I rocked my hips against him and he groaned.

It was so good to taste him again, to feel him against me, to hear him make those ardent noises. I'd begun to think I'd imagined the passion between us, to think I'd made it up, but here it was all over again. It was real, totally real.

My hands flew to his waistband. I fumbled with the metal button, my fingers clumsy with urgency. Gage took his hands off my ass to help me.

The doorbell rang.

He growled against my mouth. His arms tightened around me as he plunged his tongue desperately into me. I did the same to him, the need I felt for him almost painful in its intensity. Whoever it was outside the door could stuff it.

The doorbell rang again.

He withdrew his mouth from mine with a short, rueful laugh. I blinked up at him, stunned.

"Wha—" I said incoherently.

"The food is here." He grinned at me.

I'd forgotten the food. "Shit. Damn it."

He pressed his forefinger against my lower lip, pulling it down slightly. "I'll get the door. Don't worry, I'm not done with you."

I climbed off his lap, pouting. Gage laughed again, ruffling my hair. He stood up, started toward the door.

"Shouldn't I answer?" I said. "Don't you want to stay incognito?"

"Yeah, good idea."

He leaned against the wall next to the door as I opened it, handing me a fifty to pay the delivery girl. She gave me the food and rummaged in her pouch for the change.

"She can keep it," Gage said softly.

"Keep the change," I said.

The girl's eyes widened to circles. "Are you sure?"

"Yeah," I said. "Have a good night."

She wished me the same with the biggest smile I'd ever seen on a delivery person's face. I shut the door and turned to Gage, my hands full of white paper bags.

"That was generous."

He shrugged. "It was nothing. They work hard and don't make much."

I just smiled. "Let's eat."

We'd ordered a feast, and the containers as I opened them released a marvelous perfume of Indian spices and ghee. Normally, that smell would conquer almost anything else in my mind, it was so intoxicating. I swear Indians can make anything taste good, even concrete. But tonight I wasn't feeling it.

Oddly, my encounter with an invisible assailant hadn't managed to kill my appetite, but lust for Gage did. My food tasted delicious. I just wasn't very interested in it.

"Aren't you going to eat?" he said.

I poked at my lamb biryani without enthusiasm. "It's good, but I think I'm going to eat it later."

"Too worried to eat?" he said softly.

"No. Too horny."

He choked, snorted, laughed.

"What?" I said innocently.

"You kill me." He shoved his food away, still chewing. "Let's come back to this. We've got something more important to do."

Chapter 9

Joy

Gage stood up, his hip bumping the table and knocking one of the paper bags to the floor. I jumped out of my chair and went for him, giving a little hop as he grasped my waist. He lifted me and I threw my legs around his waist.

"I don't know how I made it this long without you," he said, kissing me again.

The ugly suspicion he'd been with other women nagged at my mind. I put it away. Maybe he had. Maybe he hadn't. Right now, we were together and I was going to make the most of it.

"Bedroom," he mumbled against my lips.

I pointed over his shoulder at the truncated hallway that contained my bathroom and bedroom. Gage turned, with me still in his arms, and headed toward the bedroom. Damn, he was strong, especially now he wasn't sick. He carried me as if I didn't weigh anything.

He strode into the bedroom and tossed me on the bed. I bounced.

"Take off your clothes," he said.

If Barry had given me an order like that, it would have pissed me off. When Gage did it, I got excited. I tore at my clothing, throwing garments any which way on the floor.

"You're overdressed," I said.

He yanked his T-shirt over his head and shucked off his jeans. Then he stalked to the bed, prowling toward me with the unconscious grace I'd only glimpsed in the cabin. When he got to me, I spread my legs to make room for him and clasped him around the waist, my ankles locking against his back.

"You don't waste time," he said with a naughty grin.

"I don't want you to escape before I have my wicked way with you."

He lowered himself on top of me, naked male chest to my bare breasts. "What if I don't want to escape?" He bit me lightly on the side of my neck.

"All the better." I turned my head and captured his mouth again.

My hands trembled as I buried my fingers in his thick, soft hair. It was a combination of lust, sexual frustration, and ... joy, I suppose. Joy. He was back again, at least for a little while.

He groaned. "God, I love the taste of your mouth. I want to taste you everywhere."

That was all right with me.

"I want to taste you, too."

He pulled off me, giving himself enough room to cup a breast in his big, calloused hand. "First these."

His hand kneaded me, thumb brushing over my eager nipple, and I arched my back, pushing myself up into his hand. My body hurt, I wanted him so much. And he gave himself to me, lavishing the attention of his hands and mouth on first one and then the other of my breasts.

Finally I pushed him away, urging him to lay on his back. I bent my head to his chest and licked his skin. He sighed, a hand coming up to stroke my hair as I continued to kiss him.

His skin felt deliciously warm beneath my lips. I smelled a hint of sweat on him and it excited me. I loved the raw smell of his body, no cologne or anything else to distract me from him.

I thought I'd never see him again and now he was here, his bare skin warm and delicious against mine, his big body trembling beneath my kisses. It was almost more than I could bear. I sighed as I pressed my lips to his chest, the soft curling hair, the hard male nipples.

His fingers moved restlessly through my hair. "Nova."

"Yeah?" I paused in my kissing.

"I need you."

"You've got me."

He tugged at my upper arms. "Come up here. I need to taste you."

I let him urge me back up to his mouth. He kissed me voraciously, his hand finding its way back to my breast.

"God, I missed these," he muttered against my mouth.

I giggled.

"You're breaking that promise again." He nipped my lower lip.

I grabbed his head and plunged my tongue into his mouth. My hands stroked and caressed everywhere I could reach—his hair, the back of his neck, his hard shoulders and the flat planes of his back, the long indentation of his spine. My skin was hungry, starving, for the touch of his. He felt so good beneath my palms, against my thighs, his stiff cock shoving against me as if it couldn't contain itself.

Gage rolled onto his back, taking me with him so I ended up draped across him. "Sit on my face."

"What?" I laughed a little.

"Ah ah, Miss Pennyman. No laughing. Just do it." His blue eyes looked almost black in the low light of my bedroom as he pulled me farther up his body.

"You talk dirty, Dalton."

He gave me a lopsided grin. "And you like it. Turn around."

I frowned, puzzled.

His grin widened. "Sixty-nine, Pennyman. Ever heard of it?"

Whoa. He wanted me to—while he—I'd never done that before. I blinked down at him.

"Go on." He smacked my ass.

Bossy man. But okay, I could play along. I turned around, pointing my rear end right at his face. This couldn't be a good thing. I glanced over my shoulder at him, unsure.

"Yeah," he growled. "That's what I'm talking about. Put your knees on either side of me."

I did as he instructed. His big hands spread me apart, fingers curving around the sides of my hips. He pulled me down toward his face.

A hot, wet tongue slid right up my center. I gasped. He did it again and I moaned.

This position put my face right at his cock. I took it in one hand. Damn, it was hard as steel and it twitched when I touched it.

The musky aroma of aroused male made my sex throb with need. I had a crazy urge to rub myself against him, and he was busy licking me in every conceivable pattern. So I put my face against the tender skin of his inner thigh, rubbing my cheek against him.

Then I used my other cheek to rub his ball sack. He sighed. Apparently, he liked what I was doing, so I did it some more. And then I licked him thoroughly, everywhere I'd already put my face. He was even hotter down here than all those other places I'd kissed him.

His licking was driving me crazy. My pussy ached for him, and every caress of his tongue both satisfied and fed that ache. I had to get him inside me, but first I wanted to make him as insane with desire as I was.

Finally, I took his cock in my mouth, drew my tongue across the velvety tip. He was freaking huge and I couldn't get his whole length into me. The tip of him hit the back of my throat, making me gag. He groaned loudly at the same time.

He tasted like sex. I withdrew to lick the head of his cock, teasing the tiny slit at the tip, before plunging my mouth over him and taking him as deeply as I could.

"Nova," he groaned. "Turn around now."

"Nuh uh." I sucked on him.

"Jesus. Unhh—no. I wanna come in your pussy, not your mouth." He groaned again. "Stop."

Reluctantly I released him.

He lifted and turned me as if I were a doll, as if I weighed nothing, positioning me on top of him and facing forward. "Ride me."

I rubbed the head of his cock against my dripping wet folds. He moaned, his eyes going even darker than before, his perfect lips swollen and parted. I pushed him into the entrance of my sheath. He grabbed my ass and shoved me down onto him, impaling me with sudden, agonizing pleasure.

My head fell back as I shouted.

"How's that?" he said between gritted teeth.

"Good." I ground my hips against him, whimpering at the pleasure of the contact of my pelvic floor with his body. "So good."

"Yeah?" He lifted me up and dropped me, impaling me all over again.

"Oh, Gage! Yeah!"

I had neighbors now, unlike when we were isolated at the cabin. But I didn't give a damn who heard me. I had Gage buried deep inside me and it felt so good I couldn't control the sounds I made. All I could do was rock up and down on top of him, sobbing with the pleasure of it.

He was huge and I was tight. I hadn't done anything for release since I'd lost him. The pressure and stretching and dragging of his cock against the walls of my sheath felt so intense that my eyes rolled back in my head.

I forgot everything else in my life. There was nothing but me and him and our bodies joined. Nothing but this moment, this pleasure. I shattered in ecstasy with him inside me and I never wanted it to end.

"I can't—" he gasped. "Can't—"

His hips slammed upward against mine, his arms worked me up and down on top of him, his face tense with his passion, dark gaze fixed on me. The bed squeaked. My tits bounced rhythmically with the force of his loving.

"Let go," I said. "It's all right."

Just as the words left me, the pleasure inside my body mounted again. I whimpered, rising and falling over him as he groaned and shook beneath me. His mouth opened wide, as if he couldn't get enough air. His hands pounded my hips down onto him, over and over, our flesh slapping together noisily.

He shouted my name. Flooded me with wet heat. I shuddered and cried out as another, smaller orgasm overtook me.

Then, panting, I collapsed on top of his heaving chest. His arms came around me, holding me so tightly. So tightly. I laid my cheek against his sweaty skin and clasped him to me as his heart thundered beneath my ear.

"You're the best thing that's ever happened to me," he said. Then he laughed. "God, that's a lame cliché. But it's true."

"I don't mind clichés if they're true." I kissed his throat. "And I feel the same way about you."

This was safer than talking about love, I guess. Neither of us had to risk using that L-word. I liked hearing that I meant a lot to him, though. It was good. It was something, anyway.

"I want you to know I haven't been with anyone else since I met you." He caressed my hair.

That was good, especially since in the heat of the moment I'd forgotten to ask about condoms. In a moment of optimistic insanity, I'd had my birth control patch renewed, so I was covered there. I guess the renewal hadn't been as crazy as I'd thought.

"Nova?"

"Hmmm?"

"What about you?"

I raised my head to give him a puzzled look. "What about me?"

He licked his lips. "Have you been with anyone?"

"Seriously?"

He gazed at me, his eyes way too somber considering we'd both just come hard and fast. "Seriously. Have you?"

"No. Of course not."

His brows drew inward and up at the same time, an expression that almost seemed like a trademark of his. "What does that mean?"

I slapped him lightly across his left delt. "It means I lo—care about you. It means I wasn't over you, even though I tried to be. Of course I wasn't seeing anyone."

He studied me, his gaze traveling back and forth across my face as if searching for clues I might be hiding something from him. Then he smiled bashfully, looking both vulnerable and pleased. "Really?"

"Yes, damn it. Did you think I'd forget you the minute you flew off in that stupid helicopter?"

His face fell. "I shouldn't have left."

"That's not what I mean. Well, it is, sort of, but—what I'm trying to say is that other guys don't interest me."

The smile reappeared. "Good."

"You look unbelievably smug right now."

He just grinned even more widely. "I'm relieved that some local dude didn't get to you before I could come back and make things right."

"I see." I raised my brows. "And you're absolutely sure you haven't been with anyone either?"

He sobered as he reached out to touch my face. "Absolutely. I didn't want anyone else. I couldn't stop thinking about you."

"I thought you didn't want me anymore," I confessed.

"Baby, that will never happen." His eyes were so serious, so real, and I wanted to believe him. I really did.

"Never?" I drew my chin back skeptically. "Never is an awful long time."

"I know. I don't want to be too intense here, but you mean a lot to me." He brushed a strand of hair off my cheek. "The only reason I left was because of The Deal. I wanted to protect you."

He was still inside me, but I leaned up, stretching to press a kiss to his mouth. "We're in it together now. You and me."

"Nova—"

"You and me, Gage. I'm not going to let you face this thing alone."

Chapter 10

Don't Help Me

Gage:

Nova's bedroom was almost as bare-bones plain as her living room. It contained the bed, a dresser that looked like it had come heavily discounted at the thrift store, and nothing else except a retro-style lamp on top and an alarm clock. The ceiling had that popcorn texture that looked more like somebody had stuck mashed potatoes all over the Sheetrock than like actual popcorn.

But the room didn't need anything else because she was in it. Her warm body lay spooned against me, her round ass pressing against my groin. I held her to me with an arm around her waist. Her hair smelled like vanilla. No woodsmoke anymore.

Nova Pennyman was by far the sweetest, sexiest girl I'd ever known. And she hadn't kicked me out, so I must have a chance with her. Not a chance to get laid, as that had already happened. A real chance at something more, something long-lasting.

Normally, as I said before, chicks throw themselves at me. Before Nova, I never even had to try. That kinda embarrassed me now. What an over-privileged ass I'd been, assuming any woman I wanted would be ready to fall on the nearest bed with her legs open for me.

Not that I'd been cruel or even neglectful to the women I'd had. When I was with a woman, I took care of her, made her feel really good. It was a point of pride; I enjoyed seeing them enjoy themselves; and their enhanced pleasure made the whole encounter better for me. But the arrogance in my assumptions now made me want to cringe.

Nova hadn't been like that. She'd made me work. That, and the fact we'd both been really sick when we met, had forced me to get to know her as a person before I managed to seduce her. And now I was caught, utterly tangled up in her, and I didn't even want to get free.

I glanced down at her sleeping face. She'd dozed off after our third round, but for some reason I still couldn't sleep. Too many worries floating around in my skull.

I slipped carefully out of bed, making sure not to wake her, and padded back into her tiny living room. This apartment wasn't much. Shabby, old, tired, and almost un-furnished, it looked pretty much the way I'd always imagined a college student apartment to look. Minus the centerfolds tacked to the wall and the beer-bottle collection. It even smelled old.

I found my leftover dinner and sat down with it at the dining-room table, a piece that looked at least two decades older than the apartment building. It was old enough to be retro-cool. It had a red Formica top and silvery metal banding around the skirt.

What were we going to do now? Would she let me move in with her?

I hadn't even gotten myself a hotel room, I'd been in such a hurry to find her. Then when I'd gotten to her place and she wasn't here, I hadn't wanted to leave in case she showed up again. So I'd camped out on her front step and waited. And waited.

All that waiting had made me ravenous. I'd forgotten about it in the heat of her body, but now it was back in a big way. I needed food, stat.

When I'd seen her coasting up on her bike, the relief had been stunning. As in, I'd almost lost my ability to speak for a second. After that crazy dream, part of me had been sure she was ... dead. Maybe something even worse than dead.

Now I had her peacefully sleeping in the other room and it was taking all my self-control not to bring the food in there to eat. Just so I wouldn't have to let her out of my sight.

It would kill me if something bad happened to her. Kill me.

I paused in stuffing tandoori chicken into my face as rage suddenly swamped me. *He* was the cause of this. Him and my mom. What right had he to take away the one chance at happiness I'd ever had? What right had he to terrorize an innocent woman, to make her feel unsafe in her own home? She deserved to feel, to be, safe.

I was being irrational. The devil doesn't give a shit about rights, or moral conduct. If he did, he wouldn't be the devil.

Still, it enraged me to think he could continue in this vein indefinitely, tormenting Nova until she went crazy.

"Gage?" Her soft voice came from the hall behind me.

I turned in my chair. "Shit, I'm sorry. I didn't mean to wake you up."

"You didn't. Anyway, I'm starved. What's for dinner?"

She wore an old, worn flannel robe, pink with a pattern of roses all over it. Her dark hair stuck out in several different directions, adorably rumpled. I slid my arm around her waist and tucked her against my side.

"I like your outfit," I said, turning my head and nipping at her waist through the threadbare flannel.

"Oh, God," she said, covering her eyes. "I forgot what I was wearing. I'm sorry."

"Don't be. It's cute."

"It's granny wear. My mom gave it to me for Christmas and I felt guilty about not liking it so I wore it anyway."

"Baby," I said, biting her again. "You could wear a dress made of those giant black garbage bags and you'd still be sexy."

She gave me a shove, laughing. "No way."

"Way." I tugged at her waist. "Sit down and eat."

Nova slid into the other chair. "There's something I forgot to tell you."

"Oh?" I said, sticking a piece of naan—Indian bread—into my mouth.

"Yeah. Right before the demon or whatever showed up, I saw Jeremy again. He was standing outside the art building."

I stopped chewing to stare at her. "You saw Jer?"

"Yeah."

"You sure it was him?"

She nodded as she stuck a fork in her lamb. "Yep. I know I only saw him once, but it was memorable. He was wearing the same clothes."

"Shit. Wonder what it means?"

"I don't know." She chewed her lamb thoughtfully. "Maybe he was trying to warn me? Help me?"

"Or maybe he attacked you," I said darkly, my anger rising again.

"You think so? He didn't seem like that kind of guy."

"He wasn't in life. But I don't know—maybe death changes you."

Nova sighed, tilting her head. "Gage, I'm pretty sure it wasn't Jeremy who attacked me. I think he's up to something else; I just don't know what."

I flashed on the bum in the alley, the one whose brown eyes had seemed blue for an instant. "I thought I saw him too, not long ago, but it was different. I was talking to this guy and it was like his eyes changed for a second, became Jeremy's eyes."

Nova pulled her chin back. "Freaky."

"Yeah. For real. It was just a second, though, and then it was gone." But he'd gotten me to take the guitar, and he'd called me G.

"He gave me that guitar," I said, gesturing toward the instrument.

"He did?" She frowned at it, then looked quizzically back at me.

"This homeless guy, he had that guitar. I passed him on the street and he tried to get me to take it. I wouldn't, until I saw his eyes." I shook my head, rubbing at my eyebrows. "God, I sound like a psycho."

"No, you don't. Or maybe we're crazy together." She grinned at me, obviously trying to lighten the mood.

"I think that goes without saying."

"Where are you going to spend the night, Mr. Dalton?" she said, still smiling. "Do you have a hotel room?"

"I can get one if you want me to," I said.

"No. I mean, I'd love it if you stayed with me. Except—" She glanced around at her living room with a rueful grimace. "I don't have much."

"I was hoping you'd ask me to stay," I said.

Her lips parted. "You were?"

Did she not understand how much I wanted her? How much I needed to protect her?

"I wouldn't let you be alone tonight, because of whatever attacked you. But even if that hadn't happened, I'd want to be with you."

Her face fell. "The only reason you're here is that dream you had. If I hadn't been in trouble, you wouldn't have come."

The look on her face was killing me. I reached across the table and grabbed onto her hand. "Nova, if it hadn't been for that goddamn Deal, I wouldn't have left you. We'd probably still be up at the cabin, maybe snowed in all over again."

She gave me a tentative smile. "Really?"

"Really."

"That sounds pretty good, actually."

I squeezed her hand. "I'd like nothing better than to be snowed in with you. But I have to find a way out of The Deal before you get hurt for real."

She straightened her back, a determined light in her amber eyes. "I'll help you."

"Nuh uh." I shook my head. "You stay out of it. I don't want you getting into any dangerous situations."

"But I've already been in a dangerous situation. What difference would it make if I helped out?"

I did not like the way she was looking at me. It reminded me all too vividly of our time in the cabin, when she bossed me around so ferociously. She had that same gleam in her eye, the same stubborn set to her jaw.

"Nova, if you get any more involved, he'll have even more reason to come after you. We don't want to give him that."

She shook her head at me. "If you think I'm going to sit around on my butt while you're in trouble, you're crazier than I thought."

"I'm crazy about you. If he really hurt you, I'd—I couldn't stand it, Nova. I don't want that to happen. Promise me you'll stay out of it."

Her eyes drooped at the corners, her mouth turning down. "I can't. Because if you got hurt, it would kill me."

Damn. I sighed and held out my arms. Wordlessly, she got up from her chair and came over to me and straddled me. I wrapped my arms around her tiny waist as she looped hers around my neck and rested her head on my shoulder.

"I don't know how I can feel so much for you when we've only spent a week together," I murmured against her hair. Then I cringed. "That sounded shitty. What I meant was—"

"I know," she interrupted. "It seems like it shouldn't be possible."

Did she still love me?

"I'm going to stay in Avery's Crossing," I said. "I want to be with you, keep seeing you. That was what I meant earlier."

"Okay." She kissed the side of my neck. "That would be amazing."

"Yeah?"

"Yeah. Mind-blowing."

I laughed. "Mind-blowing, huh? That sounds pretty good. Intense."

"Exactly."

"The thing is, I'd like to live with you. I want to make sure you're safe. Or if you don't want that, I can have a security team here for you."

"I'd rather have you."

I was hoping she'd say that.

Chapter 11

Guard Dog

Nova:

On Monday morning, I packed up my watercolor gear in preparation for my class. Gage had declared he would go with me to make sure I was safe. It seemed like a lot of trouble for him. Sitting around and watching me paint wouldn't be a very exciting way to spend an hour, and someone might recognize him.

"You don't have to do this," I said, hefting my painting tool kit while I clutched my portfolio in my other hand.

"Yeah, I do. I'm not letting you go off by yourself." Gage took the painting tools away from me. "Besides, I want to. I want to see you on campus, doing your thing."

I smiled. "My thing?"

"Your student thing. The stuff you do when I'm not around. I want to get to know you."

That was so sweet I went up on my toes to kiss him. My hand lingered on his stubbled jaw. "Okay, then. Let's go." Then I frowned. "You don't have a bike, do you?"

"Not here."

"Crap."

He grinned. "It's not a problem. I have a car, remember?"

"Yeah, but parking on campus is really tight. Like, there isn't any. Taking a car is more trouble than it's worth."

"How about we park close by and walk? Would that work?"

"Aren't you afraid of being seen?" I said, thinking of herds of screaming college girls.

"I'm never afraid," he said with a cocky tilt of his chin. "Except when I'm worried about you. Anyway, if we biked, we'd definitely be seen."

"Yeah, okay."

I was putting off the inevitable. When we left the apartment and ventured out into Avery's Crossing, the world would catch a peek at Gage Dalton. Before long, people would know he was in town and we'd be inundated. I'd have to share him.

Wow, shallow much?

He slung his free arm around my waist. "Nova, it'll be fine. Come on. We'll go to your class and then have some lunch."

He'd rented a nondescript blue Camry. I loaded my art stuff in the back seat and buckled myself in next to him, wishing we didn't have the gear shift between us. Gage gunned the engine and peeled away from the curb.

My hand shot out to grab the handle of the door. He took the first corner at what felt like highway speed, making me close my eyes and pray. I really didn't want to die.

He drove the next mile like the hounds of hell were right on our tailpipe. Avery's Crossing streets are pretty narrow, especially around campus, since most of them were put in during the nineteen-twenties. I'm pretty sure the original engineers didn't have this kind of driving in mind. Not to mention we were in a Camry, for crying out loud, not a race car.

After the third screeching corner, I couldn't take it anymore. "Can you slow down, please?" I said, holding on so tightly my fingers started to hurt.

He glanced sidelong at me. "You okay?"

"No. You're scaring the piss out of me."

He slowed fractionally.

"You know," I said, "if you get pulled over, you might blow your cover."

"This is going to be a problem, isn't it?" he said. "Me driving fast."

"Uh, yeah. Because I like to stay alive."

He laughed. "You sound like my mother."

"Don't even compare me with her. I don't make deals with the Prince of Hell."

Gage shook his head. "I won't let you get hurt."

"Well, the way you're driving might give me a heart attack. Turn left at the next light. We can park anywhere along here."

Still smiling, he turned sedately onto Wilson Street, an old residential street lined with charming ninety-year-old houses and huge shade trees.

"Tell you what," he said. "This afternoon I'll get a bike."

"You'd do that for me?"

He gave me a weighted look. "It's just a bike, Nova."

"Hey, bikes are expensive." But maybe not for a big movie star.

He pulled into a spot beneath a leafless maple tree and put the car in park. Then he leaned over and kissed me, nipping my lower lip. "Let's go to class."

His beard and baseball cap would help disguise him from fans ... I hoped. He didn't seem concerned at all. He just put his arm around my waist again as we walked along sidewalks broken and pushed up by huge old tree roots, his gaze traveling over the cottage-style houses we passed.

"This is a nice town," he said.

"Yeah. It is. Lots of charm."

"I like these houses."

"Really?" I said. "I would have thought you'd be an ultra-modern kind of guy."

"Nope. I like history."

There was so much about him I didn't know. I looked forward to discovering all these little details about him, like his favorite foods and what he liked to do in his spare time. Of course, I already knew he liked Indian food and playing the guitar, but I also knew there had to be a lot more to him than that.

"History," I said. "I like it too."

"Yeah?" He glanced down at me with a teasing light in his eyes. "Maybe I'll buy one of these."

I just laughed and shook my head. He wasn't serious. He'd probably only be in town for a short while, maybe a few weeks, and then he'd go back to L.A.. Leaving me behind again.

I was okay with that. He had a life to get back to, and I was in school and working, doing all that everyday stuff which I couldn't simply abandon. We both had lives to lead. But I was going to miss him painfully when he was gone.

We reached the edge of campus. Some of the girls cast lingering glances at him, and I wondered if they recognized him. Probably not, but maybe they wondered why he looked so familiar. I hoped it took everyone a good long time to figure out who he was.

I pointed to Fairchilde Hall and its giant spruce as we neared it. "That's the tree where I saw Jeremy."

He gave the spruce a long look. "He just stared at you? Didn't try talking to you?"

"No, he didn't. But I was on the porch or inside, so he would have had to yell."

We walked up the creaky wooden stairs of the building. Gage opened the front door for me. It was one of those long, narrow Victorian doors, with beveled glass in the windows, and it even still had those odd, egg-shaped brass doorknobs you sometimes see on these old houses. Inside, the smell of linseed oil immediately met our noses. I loved that smell. Normally, it instantly set me at ease, yet today there was a disturbingly dark note underlying pretty much everything around me.

This was where it had happened. The hair on the back of my neck prickled. Was he—it—still here? Was he watching us right now?

Gage glanced around at the student art on the walls. "Is this where it happened?"

"Yeah. Right over there." I pointed at the spot next to the black and ocher drawing.

It was a skeleton. Weird. At the time the attack had happened, I'd perceived all the drawings as life studies, but this...this was not life. The skull in the piece seemed to gape at me in warning.

"Jesus." He shook his head. "And nobody saw anything?"

"No. That person who came into the building never got this far. He just walked down the hall back there, like he was going into the offices."

"How do you know it was a he?" Gage said, glancing around the room.

"I don't. Just a guess."

What would have happened if no-one had showed up? I shivered, although I wore a heavy wool coat and the building was warm.

Gage's blue eyes had turned a hard slate color and his jaw was tense. "Don't come here by yourself. I want to be with you if you need to use the studio."

I bit back a sigh. Did he really think he was going to be able to follow me around like a puppy until we got the situation with his deal resolved? I loved having him near, but he was going to get sick of it. Gage wasn't cut out to be a puppy.

"Guard dog," he said, with another of those sidelong glances at me.

"What?"

"I'm your guard dog, not your puppy."

I frowned up at him. "Did I say that out loud?"

"Yes. You didn't mean to?"

"No. You're turning me even crazier than I already was." I gave him a mock stern glare before heading toward the studio.

"You can't blame me," Gage said.

"I can't? Why not?" I put a teasing note into my voice, trying to distract myself from the disturbing memories.

"Because I'm innocent, of course."

"Well, you can't follow me around everywhere. You can't come to work with me, for instance."

"Sure I can."

I stopped in the middle of the narrow hallway. Students passed us on both sides, giving us cursory glances yet somehow failing to notice who he was. Too busy with class work, I supposed.

I leaned in close. "You won't want to sit around in a boutique all day. You'll be bored out of your mind."

"You shouldn't be working right now anyway."

I glared at him. "I'm not quitting my job."

"I'll pay the rent and everything. I want you to be safe."

"No way." I shook my head. "I need that job, and it wasn't easy to find. There aren't a lot of jobs for college students with minimal experience, you know." Besides, what would I do for work when he left?

"Nova, I'll take care of you."

"I don't want you to take care of me. I want to take care of myself. You'll go back to L.A., and I'll still have to pay the rent."

"I'm not going back." He gestured toward the studio at the end of the hall, using my toolbox. "Come on, or you'll be late."

"Wait. What do you mean, you're not going back?"

He pressed his lips together, giving me a steady look. "I mean I'm not going back. I'm going to live here in Avery's Crossing."

I almost dropped my portfolio. "What? You can't do that."

"Why not?"

"Because. You can't just—your work is in California."

"Nova, actors live all over the place. I don't have to be in L.A. all the time. Let's go before you're late."

I gave him a parting glare. "We're not done discussing this."

"I know. And I'm going to win."

I ignored that remark. Students filled the studio, setting up their workspaces, filling tubs with water, getting out their palettes and tubes of paint. Voices echoed off the high ceilings and walls. The smell of linseed oil and turpentine was even stronger here—this studio was used for oil painting as well as watercolor.

I chose a table at the back, where Gage could sit next to me in an extra chair without drawing too much attention to himself. He grabbed a seat. A few of the other students glanced at him idly, but he ignored them, keeping his cap pulled low.

We were still working on the still life I'd been painting on Saturday. The professor stood in the center of the room, checking the arrangement and chatting with another student. I left Gage to run to the sink and fill my water bucket.

On my way back, the prof caught my eye. "You brought a friend?" she said.

"Is it okay? He's staying with me and he wanted to see what my class was like."

"It's fine as long as he doesn't disrupt anything," she said.

"He won't."

She studied him. "I could swear I've seen him somewhere before."

"Huh." I put as much clueless innocence into my voice as I could. "What's his name?"

Was that a cougary gleam I saw in her eye? *Back off, artist lady.*

"Robert," I said. Gage was his stage name, so it was true, although misleading, since he never used Robert.

"Hm. Okay, well, don't let him distract you from your work."

I returned to my desk and finished setting up my tools. My painting was still taped to my drawing board; all I had to do was lay it out on the desk. Gage studied it while I pondered what I was going to do next. All it really needed was some emphasis on the darks and maybe a little white gouache to bring out a highlight or two.

A pure watercolor uses translucent watercolor paint only, holding out the white of the paper for the highlights, but my prof didn't mind if we added a bit of gouache or acrylic as accents.

"I still have that drawing you made of me," Gage said.

I glanced at him. "Yeah?"

"I framed it and hung it by my desk." He held my gaze, almost like he was trying to tell me something else, communicating subtext through his eyes.

"I still have the others," I said, squeezing some Prussian blue out of the tube and onto my palette. "In fact, I started a painting based on one of them."

His eyes crinkled. "You did?"

"Yep. I'll show it to you later."

He looked remarkably pleased by that news.

Chapter 12
Classy

Nova:

I put my piece away in the flat file reserved for my work. Then Gage and I left, apparently without anyone recognizing him. The professor continued giving him long looks, though, even as we left the studio.

"I think she suspects," I whispered as we walked through the student gallery.

"Yeah?"

"It won't be long before she figures you out." I opened the door and we walked onto the front porch.

The air smelled like Christmas because of the spruce tree. A bird trilled from somewhere high in its branches. Misty, filtered light made the day bright even though the sky was gray.

On the sidewalk, throngs of students charged along on their way to their next class. None of them seemed to notice us, which gave me a little relief. The chatter and busyness of the campus almost felt like a bubble shielding us from the attention we would eventually receive.

He shrugged. "It has to happen sometime."

"You're not worried?"

He put his arm around my waist. "My security team is coming in on Saturday. In the meantime, we'll keep a low profile. Where do you want to eat?"

"Wherever. Pizza is fine."

I glanced around the front landscaping, which consisted mainly of still leafless azaleas growing at the feet of the monster spruce, and paused. A man stood on the sidewalk, beneath the canopy of the enormous spruce. It wasn't the exact spot where Jeremy had been, but it was within a yard.

This guy had on a black suit, which looked a little strange on campus. Hardly anyone wore suits there, except a few people in admin. The cigarette in his hand gave off enormous clouds of sweetly spicy smoke that didn't smell like tobacco at all.

Wait a minute—that was the same guy I'd seen when I was getting coffee with Skylar. He was looking right at me, too. Just like he'd been that other day...

I shivered and grabbed Gage's hand.

Gage glanced down at me. "You okay?"

"Nova?"

Skylar's voice made me turn around, Gage swinging around with me. She stood at the foot of the Fairchilde steps, wearing a Mad Men-style pencil skirt with a short, snug cardigan, her crimson hair rolled into an exaggerated pageboy style. Her eyes were heavily lined cat-eye fashion with black liquid eyeliner and her lips were as red as her hair.

Sky frowned at me, looking puzzled. She studied Gage with squinty eyes and I wondered if she could tell who he was.

"I thought you weren't seeing anyone," she said in a suspicious tone.

"I wasn't. Now I am."

She gave an unpleasant laugh. "And here I thought you were trying to get Barry back."

"I don't want him back."

Gage sent me an inquiring glance. "Is this..."

"My ex-roommate, Skylar."

"The boyfriend thief," he said, descending the stairs with me in tow.

Skylar's mouth fell open. "You told him? Who is this guy, anyway? Have I met you before?"

"I doubt it," he said. "I've gotta thank you, though, for taking Barry out of the picture so I could have Nova."

"I know your voice." She took a step closer in her pointy-toed pumps, her eyes narrowing to gimlet pinpricks. "I know I've seen you somewhere before."

I didn't know what to do. It was Gage's call whether or not to reveal himself to her, but I thought it might be better if he did rather than waiting for her to figure it out on her own. That way, we'd have a chance of controlling her reaction.

I threw a glance over my shoulder. The man in the suit was gone.

Gage stuck out a hand. "You cannot tell anyone or make any noise," he said. "I'm Gage Dalton."

She took his hand with a blank stare. Then her mouth fell open and her eyes went so wide I could see whites all around the brown of her irises. "No. Way."

"Yeah," he said.

She stared first at him, then at me. "How? What? I don't understand."

I really did not want to share this moment with Skylar. Yeah, I'd fantasized about her finding out, but now the moment had arrived it seemed to cheapen what Gage and I had. But it was too late.

"We met in Subalpine," I said. "Where my parents' cabin is."

"Oh, my God." She started to bounce on her toes. "Oh, my God."

"Skylar, stop," I snapped. "We don't want anyone to know he's here."

"I can't believe this," she said in a ridiculous, breathy voice as she gazed worshipfully at him. "Gage Dalton. I can't believe it."

"Why don't we drop you wherever you're going?" Gage said.

I glanced at him and he winked. I wasn't sure what he was trying to tell me with that. He didn't seem particularly upset by Skylar's reaction to him, so I guessed all was well.

"Oh, my God," she said again. "That would be so, so amazing. I'm your biggest fan. Seriously. Oh, my God! I've seen every one of your movies."

"Skylar!" I glared at her.

She pressed her fingertips over her red lacquered mouth. "Oops. Sorry."

Yeah, right. Sorry my ass. She was going to squeal to anyone who would listen the instant we left her alone.

***

Gage:

Skylar chattered nonstop all the way to the car I'd rented. I mostly tuned her out as she ran on and on about all the movies I'd been in and which ones she liked the best, although all of them were "great", according to her. A sideways glance at Nova let me know she didn't care at all for her ex-roomie and was probably wishing the chick was somewhere on the surface of Mars instead of tagging along with us. I didn't blame her. The only reason I'd invited Skylar along was so I could prevent her from telling anyone about us for at least a little while.

We reached the car. I clicked the door to unlock it and the headlights blinked in response. Skylar stopped dead in the middle of the sidewalk.

"That's your car?" she said, her tone openly disbelieving.

"Yep," I said.

"But it's just a Camry."

"Uh huh. Do you want a ride or not?"

She turned suspicious eyes on me. "You're not really Gage Dalton, are you?"

"Want to see my driver's license?"

Her painted red lips tightened. "Yeah, I think I would." She sent a sharp glance at Nova.

"You don't have to prove anything to her, Gage," Nova said.

"It's okay." I took out my wallet and flipped it open, extending it to Skylar. "See? I'm the real thing."

77

She leaned over, studying it minutely. A narrow-eyed glance up at me, then another scan of the license. "Hm. Maybe it is you."

"Why would he lie?" Nova said.

"I don't know. Maybe because you're playing a practical joke on me." She squinted at Nova. "You're pissed off at me because of Barry. I can tell."

"Yeah, I am," Nova said. "Because you lied to me and stole my boyfriend. But I'm over him, so whatever. I don't care enough to bother playing practical jokes on you."

Skylar's heavily painted face showed nothing but disbelief. "Uh huh."

"Are you coming with us or not?" Nova said. She looked at me. "You should have let her think we were messing with her. Then she wouldn't have anything to tell her buddies."

"Yeah. What was I thinking?" I said.

Skylar's gaze bounced back and forth between me and Nova, her penciled brows rising higher and higher. "So if you're really Gage Dalton, what are you doing with a boring car like this? What are you doing with her?"

"Did you really just say that?" I pulled Nova more tightly against my body.

"No offense," Skylar said. "It's just that Nova is so ordinary. All the other women you've been with have been ultra-glamazons, and Nova isn't like that."

"Exactly." I squeezed Nova. "That's why she's the love of my life."

Skylar's eyes became perfectly round. "The love of your life? Seriously?"

"Can we drop you somewhere, Skylar?" I clicked the unlock button on the remote key a second time, just to make the lights blink again.

"Oh. Uh, sure. Yeah, that would be great."

I opened the back door for her. She batted fake eyelashes at me as she took a seat. Nova strode around the car and got into the back seat on the other side.

"What're you doing?" I said.

"Making sure she doesn't text anyone."

"Wow." Skylar cocked her head with a sarcastic tilt. "Are you going to hold me prisoner?"

"No," Nova said. "Because then I'd have to kill you."

Skylar crossed her arms over her chest as a mulish expression took over her pretty face. She'd be a lot prettier without the exaggerated makeup. She looked like she was dressed up for Halloween.

I slid into the driver's seat. "Where to?"

Skylar rattled off an address.

"Still in the same apartment, huh?" Nova said. "Figures."

"What's that supposed to mean?" Skylar said.

"What do you think it means? You fucking stole my boyfriend and now the two of you are still living in our apartment."

"I thought you were over him."

"I am," Nova snapped. "But I guess I'm not over you."

"I said I was sorry!"

"Girls, no hair pulling or scratching," I said.

I caught Nova glowering at me in the rear view mirror. I just grinned. Her glower wobbled a little as her lips twitched with an almost-smile. Skylar stared out the window, pouting.

A few minutes later and following Nova's directions, I pulled up in front of a big, gray rectangle of an apartment building. It looked to be about thirty years old and a tiny step up from the hole Nova lived in currently.

"Thanks so much for the ride," Skylar said, opening the back door of the car. "It was such a thrill to meet you, seriously."

I turned my head to give her the most gracious smile I could manage. "Good to meet you too."

Her brown eyes turned hopeful. "Do you think I could get an autograph?"

Nova let out an exasperated sigh.

"Sure," I said.

Skylar thrust a spiral notebook at me. "Do the cover, if you don't mind."

I took the pen she offered and scribbled my name on the bright red cover of the notebook. "There you go."

"Thanks. Thank you so much."

"It was nothing. Have a good afternoon."

She took the hint and got out of the car. I watched her walk up to the building, hips wiggling in an exaggerated swivel beneath her tight skirt. Nova jumped out of the back seat and came around to the front passenger seat.

"You know she's going to text everybody the second she gets inside." She buckled her seatbelt.

When was she going to ask me about that love-of-my-life thing?

"I know," I said. "That's why we're not going out to lunch. Change of plans."

"We're not?" She scrunched up her nose. "I'm hungry."

"We'll order in. I have something to show you."

On the way out to the house, I called the real estate agent and asked her to pick up something for us to eat. I hoped Nova would like the house. Hell, I hoped I would like it. Cindy had located it and made the offer, going by the requirements I'd given her. I hadn't even seen it yet except in pictures.

I had the address in my GPS, and I followed the directions through town, toward the outskirts. I really did like Avery's Crossing. It had a classic, American small town feeling to it which, although it reminded me a little of that old David Lynch film *Blue Velvet,* also charmed me.

Big, old trees shaded the streets. They were leafless now, in winter, but in summer the place would be overwhelmingly green. Houses that looked like they belonged in kid's stories peeked out from behind the trees, their steeply pitched roofs and shutters at the windows making them almost unbearably cute. If I had the time, I'd buy one of those for real, because I knew Nova would like it. Unfortunately, we needed something immediately.

"Why are we going all the way out here?" Nova said, gazing around as the early twentieth century houses and small yards gave way to semi-rural acreage.

"I figured it would be a good place to get some privacy."

"Is there a B&B out here somewhere?" She kept scanning the misty countryside as if searching for something. A clue, maybe, as to why I'd bring her all the way out here.

"Nope." The GPS directed me to turn right onto a long, narrow, unpaved country lane which was actually the driveway of the house I'd bought.

Bushes, most of them leafless because of the winter, crowded around the edges of the long, narrow gravel driveway. They were taller than the car, and tangled with some kind of vine that made them look like jungle. A couple of crows flapped overhead, cawing loudly. The Camry bumped along the rutted surface of the lane, which clearly needed some work. I'd have Cindy get on that job immediately.

The drive curved around and a house came into view. It was only ten years old, so not the historical cottages we'd admired near the campus. But it was styled to look like a traditional farmhouse and there hadn't been much on the market, so I'd taken it.

The pictures I'd seen online had been attractive, but it was better in real life—white clapboard with a long covered porch across the front and gray shutters on all the windows. The roof was some kind of gray metal. It looked well-made and handsome, but not showy and that was good. I didn't want showy and I didn't think Nova did either.

The drive opened up to a circle shape with a small flower bed in the center. I parked the car in front of the garage. "What do you think?"

"Uh ... it's nice. Pretty. Who lives here?" She stared up at the house through the window.

"We do."

"What?" She turned her head to stare at me in obvious shock. "What are you talking about?"

"I bought it. I'm closing the deal later this week, and until then I'm renting it."

She continued to stare at me. "You bought a house? In Avery's Crossing?"

"Uh huh. Want to go in?"

"You have the key?"

I smiled at her. "The real estate agent should be here in a few. I texted her at a red light, asked her to come out here with some lunch for us."

"Wow. She's really going to do that for you?"

"People make special exceptions when you spend a lot of money with them."

"Yeah, I'll bet." She continued staring out the window, as if she had no idea what to make of all this.

"Let's look around." I opened the car door.

The air smelled incredible out here. I drew a big breath of it in through my nose. The only thing I could identify for sure was a Christmas-tree scent that probably came from all the huge evergreens along one side of the property, but there were other notes in it, too, along with a hint of woodsmoke that reminded me of the cabin.

Nova got out with a cautious expression on her face. "I can't believe you did this."

Shit. She didn't like it.

"Do you hate it?" I said, watching her.

"No, I don't hate it. It's beautiful. But—" She stopped and rubbed her forehead. "I'm not sure what I'm supposed to do here. You just came back to me. We haven't known each other very long, and already you're buying a house and expecting me to move in with you."

"Baby, we already talked about this. I can't protect you if we're living across town from each other."

She crunched across the gravel to me, hands stuck in her jeans pockets. "I know. And I appreciate what you're trying to do. It just scares me."

"Am I moving too fast?"

She dropped her gaze to the ground. "A little."

The last thing I wanted to do was scare her, but her reluctance was starting to scare me. If she pulled away, if she left me, I didn't know what I'd do. Besides missing her miserably, that was.

"Would it help if you had your own room? And you can keep your apartment. You don't have to give up anything. I just want to be sure you're safe."

Slowly, she lifted her head and met my eyes. "Yeah. Okay, that could work."

All right. We were making progress. Now I just had to convince her to sleep in the same room with me.

I reached out and took her by the arms, drawing her gently toward me. "I thought you'd like this place a little better than your apartment."

She laughed a little. "It's beautiful. And huge."

"Almost four thousand square feet," I said. "But we'll have a couple security people staying here, and maybe Cindy too, so we need more room."

"Okay." She set her hands at my waist. "But you know, this feels kind of overwhelming. You're not going to start monitoring my every move, are you?"

"What?" I pulled my chin back as I stared down at her, baffled.

"You know. Like a—an over-controlling type of guy. The kind who wants to be with a girl twenty-four hours a day and starts telling her who she's allowed to hang out with."

I'd heard this story before and it gave me a chill to hear it coming from Nova. "You mean like an abuser?"

Did she really think that of me?

Her golden eyes saddened. "No. But you have to understand—I don't know you very well. I mean, in some ways I feel like I've known you forever, but in other ways I have no idea who you are. I can't allow myself to just meld with you."

"I'm not asking you to meld with me."

"Okay." She nodded. "Sure. I understand that."

"Do you?" Maybe it wasn't fair of me to be offended, but damn it's hard to hear yourself described as a possible abuser of women. "Baby, I would never hit a woman. I have no desire to control you. That's not what this is about."

She nodded, but said nothing.

"You know I never even spent the night with a woman before you? I sure never asked anyone to live with me. This is new to me, too."

"You never spent the night with a woman? Not even once?"

"Not even once. I never even took a nap with one until you." I laid my hand against the side of her beautiful, elfin face, stroking her temple with my thumb. "I'm learning this stuff as I go along. I never want to scare you. Ever. If you need to live in your apartment, I guess I can handle that, but I might have to post a security guard there. Otherwise, I'll never be able to sleep."

Chapter 13
Girlfriend

Nova:

The air out here smelled so clean it reminded me of the mountains and my parents' cabin. Avery's Crossing has clean air in general, but in the countryside it's even cleaner and fresher. And it was quiet. I couldn't hear any traffic noise, just some chickadees in one of the bare oak trees nearby.

I was pretty sure I'd hurt Gage's feelings when I expressed doubts about moving in with him. I didn't like hurting him, but things were moving awfully fast. On the other hand, I truly did not want to spend another night alone until we had this devil problem sorted out.

How Gage could protect me from the Prince of Darkness was unclear to me, but it didn't really matter. I needed a hand to hold. Someone to put his arms around me.

The gravel on the driveway crunched. We turned. I half expected to see a news team van or a carload of college students, but it was a dark red Lexus sedan. Probably the real estate agent.

I let myself relax against Gage's side as he hugged me against him. He was sweet to worry about me. That part touched me, maybe more than I liked to admit. He did care about me, and he was willing to compromise on the living arrangements.

A slim woman, her silver hair coiffed in a perfect bob, got out of the Lexus, two white paper bags in her hands. "Good afternoon," she said cheerfully. "You must be Robert."

Robert? I guessed he was using his legal name, Gage being the name his mom foisted on him when she made him a child actor.

"Yes, I am." He held out his hand for the food. "Here, let me take that. Thanks for taking care of it for me."

"Oh, you're very welcome." She turned her smile on me before returning it to Gage. "I'm Patty Hendricks, the listing agent for this property. Your assistant, Cindy, called me."

"Yes, I know." Gage smiled. I could see the force of that smile on Patty's face. She looked entranced, even though she apparently had no idea who he really was. "This is Nova Pennyman, my girlfriend."

His girlfriend. Wow, we hadn't even talked about that. But I guess it was implied, given we were talking about living together and we'd spent most of the past two days having sex.

"Nice to meet you, Nova." She extended her hand. "Would you like a tour or do you need to eat first?"

He glanced at me. "We'll eat, thanks."

"Okay. Let me get the door unlocked."

We followed her onto the old-fashioned wraparound porch. She retrieved the key from a box hanging from the doorknob and let us into the house.

The foyer was tastefully decorated with a console table and mirror, a travertine floor and a huge black chandelier. A few amber drops sparkled from the chandelier, which was otherwise unadorned. It was pretty conservative for a young Hollywood star, I thought.

"The kitchen is right through there." Patty pointed to the left. "I'll set myself up in the office so you two can have some privacy."

We brought the food into the kitchen, which was also country style—white cabinets, more travertine flooring, and a blue painted island with some kind of dull black stone as a counter top. An alcove-like space with a small dining room table and chairs made up the dining nook, or breakfast room or whatever they called it in a big house like this. Overall, it felt like a quality upper-middle class house, similar to the one I'd grown up in except bigger.

Gage set the food on the table. "What do you think?"

"It's gorgeous. But I kinda feel like I'm in my mom's house."

"I know, right? Nice yard, though."

The backyard, surrounded by a tall hedge of arbor vitae, was visible through the windows of the breakfast room. And there was a big pool, although it was covered at the moment.

I glanced at Gage, laughing. "A pool? In Oregon? You know it'll only be usable three months of the year if you're lucky."

"You think I should've gotten a place with an indoor pool?"

I just shook my head, still giggling.

"I didn't buy it for the pool. I bought it for the privacy." He rummaged in the bags and pulled out little paper boxes of burgers and fries. "Hope you like burgers."

"I love them." I sat down. "I'm only teasing about the pool, you know."

He glanced at me. "I know."

I took off my jacket. Something crackled in my pocket as I draped the garment over the back of my chair. I reached in and pulled out the piece of paper with Marie's name and phone number on it.

"What's that?" Gage bit into his burger.

"Something weird. I met this lady the other day. Remember how I said I'd been feeling watched? I went into this oddball bookstore. Not an occult store exactly, but it has a lot of books on meditation and auras, stuff like that. This lady came up to me and offered her help."

He squinted at me over the top of his burger. "Did she seem legit?"

"Yeah, I guess so. She didn't creep me out or anything."

"You should call her. Maybe she really can help. God knows the people I talked to didn't have anything worthwhile to say, but it's worth a try."

"I'm not sure what I'd say." Hi, do you know how to get rid of the devil? That didn't seem like a good thing to say to a complete stranger. "She told me I had something dark near me. Something dangerous."

His gaze sharpened. "That's a lot smarter and more helpful than anything I got. Maybe she really knows something useful."

"Who did you talk to?"

He shrugged. "Just a few people at some occult bookstores. Nobody seemed to believe me when I told them I was having devil problems."

"Gee, I wonder why."

"They work in occult bookstores. They should be knowledgeable." He reached out, grabbed the seat of my chair, and pulled me closer.

"What are you doing?"

"I need to be able to touch you." He picked up a fry and held it to my lips.

I bit the end off it. He'd called me the love of his life not an hour ago. Did he mean it or had he only said it to shut up Skylar? I was afraid to ask.

Patty gave us the house tour after we finished with our food. Gage reached for my hand, lacing his fingers through mine. The simple act of holding my hand made my insides flutter wildly.

It was kind of weird. I mean, we'd been all over each other for the past two days, yet I still got butterflies just because he took me by the hand. I guess two days isn't all that long, even if we had been doing little besides making love.

"Downstairs you have an office, formal living and dining rooms, family room, and mud room," Patty said as she led the way into the living room.

"Wow." I stared at the floor to ceiling windows looking out on the front yard and circular drive.

"Spectacular, huh?" she said, smiling.

"It's gorgeous."

The room also had a fireplace with a traditional mantel and paneled surround in some kind of wood, although I had no idea what it was. Beautiful, that's what. The warm wood tones and smooth grain seemed to glow in the afternoon light. I could picture a fire there in the evenings, although the room was more elegant than cozy. It wasn't as much like my parents' house as I'd first thought, because the place where I'd grown up was nowhere near as fancy as this.

And the fancy didn't stop in the living room. The family room, which I'd glimpsed when Gage and I were eating in the breakfast room, also had a fireplace. This one was in the middle of a feature wall of stacked gray stone, with a thick slab of what looked like barn wood for a mantel. An enormous, round mirror with a chunky gold frame hung above the mantel.

"Is the furniture included?" I glanced around at the pearl gray walls, casually elegant persimmon-colored sofas and cream club chairs, the modern throw rug in matching tones. Whoever had decorated it had done a beautiful job.

"Yes, it is," Patty said. "Cindy negotiated for that."

"It's lovely." I especially liked the orangey persimmon tones. They made the gray of the walls and stone seem warmer and more welcoming.

"I'm glad you like it." Gage winked at me.

I nudged him as I leaned against his side. "You know it wouldn't matter to me. I'd like anyplace you are."

"Aw," Patty said. "That's so sweet."

I blushed. My mouth had gotten ahead of me. But Gage had introduced me as his girlfriend, so my words hadn't been inappropriate. Just revealing. And he didn't seem upset at all; he was looking down at me with a smile in his eyes.

"Would you like to see upstairs?" Patty said.

"I'd love it."

"It's not the cabin," Gage said.

I peered up at him, confused. "Of course not."

"We might lose each other around here." His lips twitched.

I poked him with my elbow. "I'm pretty sure we can manage."

"You sure? We can stay in your apartment, if you'd like that better."

"Is the house not to your liking?" Patty said with a concerned frown.

"I'm just teasing her," Gage said.

I leaned into him a little more. "Is there something wrong with me keeping a little independence?"

"Not at all. As long as you don't think there's anything wrong with me bribing you to stay here with me."

"Okay, you two." Smiling, Patty strode across the glossy, wooden floor and started up the stairs. "If you need to work out your differences, I'll be upstairs."

"We're fine." Gage led me to the stairs, which were carpeted with a fine, Berber-style runner in cream and gray.

I bent down to touch the carpet. "I think this is wool."

"Is that good?"

"Yes. Very high-end. Expensive."

He shrugged. "Okay."

"You're not impressed, huh?"

"No, I like it. I'm not really into the whole interior design thing, though."

"Typical guy," I said, caressing the carpet.

"You keep touching it that way, I'm gonna be jealous."

I laughed. "That's weird and a little kinky."

"Come on." He tugged on my hand. "I want to see where we'll sleep."

I let him draw me upward. The stairs had an elegant curve to them, and white-painted balusters with a handrail that matched the floors. It was so beautiful that I found it hard to imagine myself living here. The cabin in the woods had been totally my speed; this was something else.

"What's your place in L.A. like?" I said.

"Two story, no yard. The complex has a pool." He shrugged. "I don't know. It's a luxury condo. I had it professionally decorated, so I guess it's pretty slick."

"Oh, yeah?" We reached a small landing, decorated with a painting, a Bombay chest and a small chair.

"Venetian plaster," Gage said.

"Huh?" I looked around and saw nothing that looked like Venetian plaster.

"In my condo. The decorator insisted I needed a wall of Venetian plaster. It's this odd blue-gray color."

"I don't think this house has anything like that."

He shook his head, obviously pretending to be concerned. "I'm not sure I can take it then."

I stuck my tongue out at him. "I'm falling in love with this place already, so you'd better take it."

What was I saying? I was supposed to keep a prudent distance, be sensible, be careful. I didn't want to allow him to control me; I wanted to remain independent. And here I was already planning to move in. I could hardly wait.

Gage merely leaned over and kissed me, open-mouthed, making me pant. "That's what I want to hear."

We reached the second floor. A balcony overlooked the foyer on one side and part of the living room on the other. On one end of the upstairs hall were three regular bedrooms, each with its own bath. On the left was the master, entered through six-panel double doors.

The room already contained an enormous, king-size sleigh bed with a padded bench, upholstered in a zebra print, at its foot. On one wall hung a large Venetian mirror, so there was the Venetian touch we were so worried about. I glanced at Gage with a smirk. He wouldn't know or care about the style of the mirror. I, on the other hand, loved every beveled edge of it.

The bed linens were all in snowy white, the curtains in a black and white stripe. A fluffy white rug lay over the pale wood of the floor and a black, French-looking chandelier sparkling with clear crystal drops hung from the center of the cathedral ceiling.

"Elegant," I said. It looked like a layout in some upscale shelter magazine.

"Is that zebra?" Gage pointed at the bench. "And a chandelier. God, it's got a chandelier."

"Yep." I grinned at him. "Glamorous enough for you? Or should we have some plaster installed?"

"Smartass."

"The bathroom is through here," Patty said.

The bathroom had double doors, too. Just in case you might mistake it for the walk-in closet? Both the closet and the bathroom were bigger than my entire apartment; taken together, they probably equaled the square footage of the cabin. Good grief. Who needed this much space? Not that I was complaining. No, sir.

"This is like a temple of bathing." I stared at the giant soaking tub with its marble surround and view over the back yard.

Another chandelier hung over the tub, the smaller sibling of the one in the bedroom. The other fixtures in the room were more modern and sleek, which was probably good for Gage or he might have felt overwhelmed with the sheer feminine glamour of the place.

"So is it satisfactory?" Patty said.

"Absolutely." Gage smiled at her. "Thanks for bringing us lunch and showing us around."

They shook hands and chatted about the closing while I wandered into the walk-in closet. My God. I could have set up a lovely living room in here, except for the lack of windows. It had been fully furnished with built-in shelving and drawers, including a bank of tiny ones that seemed to be intended for jewelry. A small chandelier like the one in the bathroom hung in the center of the room, with smaller sconces on the walls and flanking the full-length mirror. An island lay beneath the chandelier. The island had niches and shelves and a padded bench. I'd never seen anything like it in real life.

Hard, male arms slipped around me from behind. Gage lifted my hair and kissed the back of my neck. "Think you could make do with this?"

"God, Gage, it's so much more than I've ever had. I'm—I don't even know what to say."

"Say you like it and you'll stay with me here."

I turned around and put my arms around his waist. "I love it and I'll stay with you here." Then I frowned. "But how will I get to work and class?"

"I'll have one of the guys drive you, or I'll take you."

"You know that's not necessary."

He frowned. "Yes, it is. I want you to be safe."

"But what are they going to do if he decides to—you know—get me?"

"I don't know. But you said he hasn't attacked you when other people are around. So it's a start."

"I don't want to depend on you for everything."

"Baby, it's only for a little while, until we figure things out. Please do this for me."

I sighed. Shook my head. "I'm worried."

"Don't be."

"But—I love this house. I really do. And I lo—care for you. A lot. But I need to have my own transportation. Otherwise, I feel helpless."

"I'll get you a car."

"No! Gage, no. You shouldn't do that. I don't want your money or gifts from you or—" I hung my head. "I don't want you to ever feel like you're buying me."

"What?" He sounded both shocked and offended. "Why would I think that? I know that's not who you are."

"I feel like I'm at a major disadvantage here. Powerless."

He pressed his forefinger to the center of my lower lip. "You are not powerless."

I sucked his finger into my mouth and lightly bit down and he drew in a sharp breath, his eyes going dark.

"You're treading on dangerous territory, there," he said, his voice husky. "Patty might have to show herself out."

"Robert? Nova? I'm going to leave the keys on the dining room table," Patty called from the doorway.

"Her timing's perfect," I said.

"Thanks, Patty," Gage yelled over my head.

We listened to her footsteps retreating down the hall, then the stairs, then through the lower level of the house. Finally, the front door shut.

"Time to break in this bed," Gage growled against the side of my neck. Then he bit me.

I moaned. Our mouths fused as our hands roamed feverishly, tearing at clothes, touching everything we could reach.

Chapter 14
Black Suit

Gage:

The bed would definitely work. It was big enough for almost any kind of sexual position or game I knew. The mattress was soft enough for sleeping comfort, but firm enough for good leverage during a hard fuck session.

Although the hedges outside didn't come up past the window level, plantation shutters covered the glass so we had enough privacy to screw our brains out in the middle of the day without anyone watching. The light flooding in through the shutters lit up my girl's face and her gorgeous, completely edible body.

The room was way too girly, but I liked the black and white, so I could live with it. I could tell Nova loved it by the way her eyes sparkled every time she looked around. It was worth putting up with glitzy mirrors and chandeliers to see that look on her face.

At the moment, those gorgeous eyes of hers were focused on her smart phone. I lay on my back, staring up at the ceiling, which I belatedly realized had been painted silver. Whoever had decorated this place had gone all out. It needed some black leather, though.

"Oh, shit," Nova said.

"What?" I rolled toward her.

"Skylar's spread the news everywhere." She held up the phone so I could see the screen. "My Twitter feed's got nothing but stuff about you and me."

"We knew it would happen, babe." I leaned down to kiss her bare shoulder. She smelled of woman and sex, and that made me hard for her all over again.

"I know, but there are pictures of you and me kissing."

I raised my head. "Huh? How'd she do that?"

"It must have been while we were walking down the sidewalk. She was behind us." She scrolled through her feed to a fuzzy picture of our lips meeting.

"She didn't even know who I was at that point."

"Yeah, she did. Remember? You told her when we were standing in front of Fairchilde."

I frowned, staring down at the picture. "Yeah, you're right. Shit. Guess we should've kept a closer eye on her from the beginning. No-one will recognize you in that shot, though, if that's what you're worried about. It's too blurry."

"That's not what I'm worried about. People will find out what I look like soon enough, if they haven't already gotten into my Facebook page. She's also saying she had you first."

"What?" I laughed. "That little skank."

"I know, right? She makes it sound like she passed you on to me."

"Whatever." Chicks made up bullshit stories about me all the time. I didn't care, as long as it didn't humiliate Nova.

"My parents are going to freak. I'd better call them." Just as the words left her mouth, her phone rang. She looked at me with raised brows. "It's them."

"Answer it."

"What am I going to tell them?"

I looped my arm around her shoulders and pulled her in against me. "The truth."

"And what is that?" She hit the talk button. "Hi, Mom."

We should have talked this out beforehand. I didn't want to confess how much she meant to me while she was talking to her mother on the phone, and I sure as hell didn't want to get into a discussion about our living arrangements now.

If I told her that I was falling in love with her, it might put her in even more danger. He might be willing to overlook a girlfriend, but not the woman I loved. For her safety, I had to keep that information to myself.

"Yeah, I'm fine," Nova said. "I figured you had. Yeah, it's true."

A muffled yet tense female voice issued from the other end of the line.

"We met in Subalpine." A long pause for more lecturing. "Because I didn't think I'd be seeing him again and also I didn't think you'd believe me." Another pause. "Well, how would I know that?"

I rubbed her upper arm. She tilted her face up and smiled at me.

"I'm staying at his place right now," she said. Yet another pause. "A house he's buying. Yes, here in Avery's Crossing."

"Would she feel better if she talked to me?" I said.

"Uh...I don't know. Mom, do you want to talk to Gage?" After another pause, she handed her cell to me.

"Mrs. Pennyman?" I said.

"Yes. Is this—is this Gage Dalton?" She sounded unsure of herself.

"Yes, it is."

"Gage Dalton the actor?"

I smiled. "Yes, ma'am. Gage Dalton the actor."

"Oh, brother," Nova muttered, rolling her eyes.

"How did you meet my daughter?"

I glanced at Nova. She was watching me, her honey-colored eyes tense. Was she worried about what I'd think of her mom, or what her mom would think about me?

"She saved my life," I said, ignoring Nova's hand clutching my arm. "I got caught in that big snowstorm in November and she gave me shelter."

"I see," her mom said slowly. Suspiciously. "And you left and didn't speak to her for six weeks?"

"That's right." Now it was my turn to be nervous. "I had something I had to take care of before I could get back to Nova."

"A wife?" Mrs. Pennyman said.

"God, no. I've never been married."

Nova clapped her hands over her eyes. I grinned at her.

"A girlfriend, then?" her mom continued.

"No girlfriend. I was single until I met your daughter. She's very important to me, Mrs. Pennyman."

"So out of the blue you just moved to Avery's Crossing and bought a house? That's a bit unusual, don't you think? You and Nova haven't known each other all that long."

"No, but we were together twenty-four hours a day for over a week. We got to know each other pretty well."

"How well?"

"Well enough to ask her to move in with me."

"Are you the reason she quit Pioneer?"

I mouthed *Pioneer* at Nova.

"Pre-med," she whispered.

"No," I said into the phone. "She'd made up her mind about that before I met her."

I could almost see her shaking her head on the other end. "It's too soon. I don't like this."

I couldn't tell her how worried I was about Nova without sounding like a nutcase, and I sure couldn't explain about The Deal.

"She's keeping her apartment," I said.

"She is? Oh. That's—uh—well, I guess that makes things a little better. What do your parents think about this?"

I smiled again, thinking of asking my mom for permission to do anything. As if she'd even care. "My mom doesn't know yet, but I know she won't have a problem with it."

"And your dad?"

My muscles tensed. That was information I didn't normally divulge to people I'd only just met, but this was different. She was Nova's mom, and I wanted her to understand, to approve. Would she think less of me because I'd never really had a father? But there was nothing I could do about it, so I plunged onward.

"My dad's not in the picture."

"Oh." A long pause. "I'm sorry. I didn't mean to be rude."

"It's okay. I don't even remember him."

"How sad. A boy ought to have a father." She sounded so genuine that I couldn't take offense.

"I got by."

"I'm sure you did. Hm. Well, all right. Put Nova back on, please. And it was nice to meet you, Gage, even if I am giving you the third degree."

"Thanks. It was nice to meet you too." That didn't sound awkward. No.

I handed the phone back to Nova. And it occurred to me that I didn't even know how old she was. Obviously, she had to be in her early twenties at the oldest, since she was still in college. Unless she'd gone to community college first. What if she'd graduated from high school early? I could be robbing the cradle.

No, her mom would have warned me off if that were the case.

Nova made some reassuring noises into the phone for a couple of minutes before hanging up. I watched her set the phone on the bedside table. The sheet slipped down, revealing her sweet, pink nipple and the bottom curve of her breast. My mouth went dry.

"She and my dad want to come visit," she said.

I tore my gaze away from her breast. "Huh?"

"They want to come down here. Meet you in person."

"Okay. We have plenty of room."

She flopped onto her back with a groan. "Not that much room. There's not enough room in the White House for us and my parents. Trust me on this."

"Okay." My gaze wandered back to her breast, drawn helplessly to that beautiful, erotic sight. "I'll put them up in a hotel."

"You're being incredibly generous about all this."

"Baby, they're your parents and they care about you. They love you. Not everyone has that, you know."

Her eyes saddened. "I know. I'm sorry."

"Don't be."

"Well, I am." She leaned against me, her naked chest pressing against mine.

I stroked her back. "I wasn't trying to make you feel guilty. Just saying you're lucky, is all."

"You're right."

The temptation was too great to resist, so I slipped my hand around to cup her. Her breast felt soft and warm in my palm, and I felt myself hardening again.

She pulled my head down for a kiss. "You're insatiable."

"Only for you."

***

Nova:

I stretched out on the bed, my arms over my head, and stared up at the amazing sparkle of the black and crystal chandelier. I'd never had such a beautiful lamp, not even in my parents' house. My mom was more the sleek and modern type. She didn't understand my girly tastes.

Someone did, though. Whoever had decorated this room had practically read my mind. The crisp black and white color scheme contrasted with the girly details made the perfect combination as far as I was concerned.

"So we need dinner," Gage said. "And I was thinking we could go out."

"People will see you." I'd been thinking I was going to have to make a fast food run, something that didn't appeal. One hamburger meal a day was enough for me.

"I made reservations. They're going to let us in the back door."

"Oh? Where?" I glanced down at my old jeans and fleece top. Not exactly the kind of outfit you wear to a restaurant that takes reservations.

"Giulia's. There isn't much to choose from in this town."

"I didn't know Giulia's even took reservations. And you're right. Unless you want pizza or Chinese food, we're kinda limited."

"They have a private room," he said. "All my stuff is at your apartment, so we'll have to go as-is."

I put my arms around his neck. "I don't want to share you with anyone."

He bent down to nip my earlobe. "Mm. I don't want to share either, but it's either that or starve. You ready to go?"

I'd just gotten out of bed after hot sex. "Are you kidding? I have to at least fix my hair."

"You look great."

I rolled my eyes ostentatiously. "I guess Hollywood guys are as clueless as regular guys when it comes to women getting ready to go out."

He just laughed. I walked into the bathroom stark naked, pretending I wasn't self-conscious at all. Spending so much time with Gage had made me less insecure about my body, since he took every opportunity to tell me how much he liked the way I looked. But I wasn't confident enough to not worry at all.

I flicked on the bathroom light and jumped at the mirror-like effect of the bare window. It looked out over the back yard and no-one had thought to put up any curtains or shades. I flicked off the light again with a muttered curse. Probably no-one could see me, since we were a fair distance from any neighbors, but it was still unnerving to walk in naked and realize I was standing in front of a bare window.

Now I had the light off, I could see it wasn't completely dark outside. The twilight gave the back yard a gloomy, mysterious quality, with long black shadows that emerged from the darkness of the hedge like a row of sentinels standing against the light spilling from the house windows.

One of the shadows moved.

I jumped again. It was still moving. I bent over the bathtub, leaning closer to the window, peering out. Was it a deer? Or had one of the paparazzi found us already? The shape of it seemed more human than animal.

Great. The media had caught us before we'd even had a chance to settle in or get comfortable with each other.

The figure meandered into one of the shafts of light coming from the kitchen. My hands pressed hard against the cold, smooth tub surround. The figure was a man in a dark-colored suit. I couldn't see anything that looked like a camera, but he was smoking. Plumes of cigarette smoke rose above his head.

I ducked down, even though he could hardly have seen me in the darkened bathroom. He hadn't even been looking in my direction. But still—a man in a black suit? In Avery's Crossing, Oregon? Not many men wore any kind of suit in this town, let alone an inky black one that fit like bespoke European garments and not some off-the-rack garbage from the discount store. I climbed in the tub so I could get really close to the window and peek over the edge of the sill.

Not too long ago, I'd seen a man in a black suit. Smoking a cigarette. Watching me. I'd bet the rest of my tuition this was the same guy.

Clutching the sill with my fingertips, I peeked out. He was still there. Still smoking. I could clearly make out the silhouette of his body. Then he turned. He lifted his chin and looked straight at my window.

Shit.

I ducked down again. Had he seen me? How was that even possible with the lights off? And what the hell was he doing in our—in Gage's— back yard?

The light in the room came on again. Gage stood in the doorway, narrow-eyed bafflement on his face. "What are you doing?"

"There's a man in the back yard."

"What?" he snapped, lunging toward the window.

"You probably won't be able to see him with the light on."

He grunted in acknowledgment and returned to darken the room. Then he leaned into the window, openly studying the yard. "I don't see anyone."

"I guess he left. He was definitely out there and he didn't look like a paparazzo."

He glanced down at me with a teasing grin. "You an expert now?"

"No. But this guy was wearing a suit. Do they usually do that?"

"Depends," he said with a shrug. "Probably not in this town, though. Too conspicuous."

"That's what I thought."

Chapter 15
Arrival

Nova:

My parents showed up on Saturday morning at the same time as Gage's security team. I looked out the upstairs window to see their familiar battleship gray SUV rolling to a stop in front of our driveway, at the same time as a second SUV—bigger and the deepest black—pulled in behind them. My parents got out, gazing around at the house and grounds. Behind them, three men jumped out of the SUV and surrounded them.

Cindy got out of the SUV after them, dressed as I remembered her in brown riding boots and skinny jeans. She had a brown suede blazer on over a cream-colored cowl neck sweater. I thought I could see a smirk on her face.

I dashed down the stairs and ran to the door. "They're here!"

"Who?" Gage called from the office slash music room.

"Everyone."

I opened the door. The security guys still surrounded my parents. They were so big I couldn't see my family, just three huge guys wearing black jackets and looking scary intimidating.

"Hi," I called out as I strode onto the porch. "I'm Nova and those are my parents."

"It's true," Cindy said. "She is Nova."

The security guys backed off a little, enough so I could see my parents' faces. This incident had not endeared Gage to them. I could see it by the irritated frowns they wore. Hadn't anyone warned the security team my parents would be here? I glanced at Cindy, wondering if Gage had delegated that task to her and she'd "forgotten."

My mom looked tiny in the midst of all those huge men. Tiny but undaunted. She had her don't mess with me, I'm a doctor face on. I kept striding, off the porch and across the gravel, while Cindy stood there and smirked.

Gage really needed to find another assistant.

My dad, on the other hand, seemed like he wanted to hit someone. I'd never seen him do that, so the glower on his face surprised me. This was not good. I didn't want him to associate Gage with overbearing security jerks.

"Hi, Mom and Dad." I waved cheerfully, as if nothing was wrong.

"Who are these people, honey?" my mom said.

"They're Gage's security team. They just got here, too, so they haven't been briefed except over the phone." Was that the right word? Briefed? I was going off military movies here, probably not the best resource.

"We apologize, Mr. And Mrs. Pennyman," said a muscle-bound blond guy who looked like he might be the leader of the pack. "It's our job to keep fans from bothering Mr. Dalton."

My mom gave him a forced-looking smile. "It's all right. I'm sure we'll recover."

My dad just continued to glower. "You need better communication between you and Mr. Dalton."

"Yes, sir."

"It's Dr. and Dr. Pennyman," I said to the security dude. "My parents are both doctors." I waved toward the house. "Come inside. Meet Gage. He was just coming down when I opened the door."

My father gave the security guys and Cindy another withering glare before turning toward the house. He wasn't going to make this easy.

You might think he'd be excited to meet an A-list star, but my dad was one of those people who thought actors were overpaid, spoiled brats who ought to get real jobs. That attitude didn't stop him from watching movies, of course, but he didn't seem to appreciate the irony there.

I faced Cindy head-on. "Hi, Cindy. Welcome to Oregon."

Her lips tightened. "Thanks a lot."

That sounded totally sincere. Not. I just smiled at her. She'd never find out how nervous she made me—not if I could help it, at least.

Gage opened the front door and came onto the porch in his stocking feet. He waved at us. The look on his face was one I recognized—the gracious actor interacts with his fans face. He couldn't be putting on a show like that for Cindy, or the security guys, who already knew him, so it must be on behalf of my parents.

I suspected it meant he was more uneasy, nervous, than he wanted to let on.

My mom and dad inspected the porch and the outside of the house as we walked up the steps. This was exactly the kind of house my mom loved, yet I couldn't read her expression at all.

Gage stuck out a hand to my dad. "Gage Dalton, Dr. Pennyman. It's good to meet you."

My dad looked him up and down before accepting the offered hand. "Is it?"

"Absolutely. You're Nova's dad." He turned to my mom. "Dr. Pennyman."

The relaxed friendliness that flowed off him probably would have fooled anyone else, but I could tell it was an act. He never behaved that way except with people he didn't know very well, and usually not even then.

My mom accepted the handshake with a smile. "Gage, it's good to meet you face to face."

"The same."

They shook. Cindy and the security team clomped up the steps behind us. Gage nodded at them and opened the door.

"Let's go inside," he said.

My palms were sweaty again. I wanted my parents to like Gage, and even more importantly I wanted them to treat him with respect. From the set of my dad's shoulders, I had an idea that wasn't going to be happening, at least not for a while.

"Where are Irene and Emily?" My little sisters loved everything about Gage. They had posters of him all over their walls.

"We left them with your Aunt Diane," my mom said. "We didn't think you two would want to be attacked by a couple of middle schoolers."

Gage looked at me and grinned. He took my hand. I noticed my parents taking note of this exchange and I waited for the parental commentary. It didn't come.

"We got a room at the Holiday Inn," my mom continued. "Thinking you'd need your privacy."

"Send me the bill," Gage said.

"Absolutely not." My dad glowered at him again. "We can pay our own way."

"Sir, I'm only trying to—"

"Look, young man." My dad confronted Gage as we entered the kitchen. "I know you're probably swimming in money and you're a hot shot actor and all that, but this is my daughter."

"I'm aware of that. I respect her and you."

Gage spoke calmly, meeting my dad's gaze with apparent ease.

"Her mother and I don't think much of this moving in business." My dad's gaze flicked briefly to me before settling back onto Gage. "She was studying to become a doctor. Did she tell you that?"

"She said she'd already made up her mind she didn't want that anymore."

My dad's brows lowered even more. "Did she? I never heard about it. She said she went up to our cabin because of a cheating ex-boyfriend. The next thing I know, she's moving back here to study art." He snorted. "Art."

Gage looked from him to me. "Her major is her decision, sir. Not mine. Or yours."

"Dad, I knew I didn't want to be pre-med when I went up there. Gage had nothing to do with it."

"You don't think he's going to be faithful, do you?" my dad said. "These Hollywood types don't know how to do anything but fool around with everything that walks past them."

I closed my eyes for an instant. "Dad, knock it off." Jeez, he'd never been this overbearing with any of my other boyfriends. "We're dating, not getting married."

"You've moved in with him."

He was starting to anger me. I let go of Gage's hand and took a step closer to my dad. "I'm twenty-two years old. If I want to live with my boyfriend, I can. I'm sorry you disapprove, but it isn't going to change anything."

"Ray, you need to lighten up," my mom said, putting a hand on my dad's arm. "Nova's a smart girl. She knows what she's doing."

Wow. That was the first time I'd ever heard anything like that from my mother. I put her changed attitude down to Gage's charm. My mom was just as vulnerable to his devastating smile as any other breathing, conscious woman on the planet.

"Gage, where would you like the guys to set up?" Cindy said from the hall behind us.

I cringed at the thought that she'd heard the exchange between my dad and Gage. My dad must have been working himself up into a state of fury all the way down here from Portland.

"The office is to the left of the foyer," Gage said. "I'll be there in a few."

"Dad, I've known for months that I didn't want to be a doctor," I said as the others filed back into the living room. "I'm sorry you're disappointed."

"Damn right I am."

"Mom is too. But I would be miserable as a doctor. It wouldn't be good for my patients."

"She's right, Ray," my mom said. "I realized that after we helped her move into her apartment. I thought you knew what was going on."

My dad just crossed his arms over his chest and said nothing. I must have gotten that habit from him. At the moment, it was obnoxious. Did I look like that when I crossed my arms?

"Gage, this is a beautiful house," my mom said. "I love this kitchen."

"I had Cindy pick it out," he said. "She did a good job. I wanted something Nova would like."

"How old are you, anyway?" my dad said, his tone still belligerent.

"Twenty-five."

"Just a kid."

"I'm an old twenty-five," Gage said. "I've been working since before I was ten."

"Acting isn't work."

Gage looked at me. I shrugged. There was no talking to or reasoning with my dad when he was like this.

"Be nice, Ray," my mom said. "Give him a chance."

I'd had enough. Maybe if I hadn't been attacked by the devil's minion, I would have been more passive, more content to let my parents dominate. But the fact was I had more pressing matters on my mind right now than whether or not my dad approved of my boyfriend's career. I couldn't explain it to them, and if I tried it would only make things worse. My dad would go ballistic if he thought Gage had endangered me in any way.

Confronting my dad was something that had always scared me. I'd never been one of those kids who smartmouthed her parents all the time. However, I wasn't going to let him get away with trying to bully Gage and me.

"You always told me a person should never go into someone else's home and insult them or be rude to them," I said, staring down my dad as my heart pounded sickeningly. "You're being rude to Gage."

"Honey, I just want to be sure he's going to treat you right."

"You can't do that by coming into his house and treating him like garbage."

"Baby, it's okay. He's just looking out for you." Gage took my hand again.

"No, it isn't." He was too much a peace-maker. "You deserve better. Dad, I don't want you and Mom here if you can't be respectful to Gage."

"Nova!" my mom protested.

"Maybe we should leave," my dad said, flexing his jaw.

"If that's the way you want it." I kept staring at him, daring him to do it, to walk out the door. "It's up to you."

"I don't want to come between you and your family," Gage said, frowning at me, his eyes troubled.

"You're not," I said. "They are."

"Young lady—" my dad said.

"Nova, that's unfair." My mom interrupted him.

"No, it's not. You're not giving him a chance. You're taking your disappointment in my career choice out on him, when he had nothing to do with it. You're not listening to me when I try to explain this to you. You're jumping to conclusions. You've come into Gage's home and tried

102

to bully him. That's so not okay I don't even know where to start, and if you can't see that then we have nothing to talk about."

"What if he hurts you the way Barry did?" my dad said. "I don't trust his intentions."

All Barry did was cheat on me. It's not like he was beating me up or anything. Did my dad think I was made of china?

"Then I'll get hurt," I said, waving my arm emphatically. "So what? Should I live my life locked in a cupboard so I never get hurt? Because I don't want to live that way."

"Barry was an idiot," Gage said, a note of steel in his voice. "I would never cheat on Nova. I'm crazy about her. I came to Avery's Crossing to be with her. That should tell you something about my intentions."

"Plus this isn't the nineteenth century. His intentions?" My voice rose. "Come on. What's next, a shotgun wedding? I'm over twenty-one, for crying out loud."

My dad's jaw kept working back and forth. He studied me, tight-lipped and angry, hands in fists at his sides. "I wanted more for you."

"More than what?"

"More than a life as a groupie who dabbles in art on the side."

"A groupie? Did you just call me a groupie?" I couldn't help it. I laughed.

His grim stare faltered. "I don't know. I thought—"

"The word is fan, not groupie," Gage said. "Since I'm not a rock star. And Nova is not a fan. She didn't even know who I was when I met her."

"I'm a fan," I said, tugging at his hand.

He shook his head, smiling at me. "You're a terrible liar."

"I'm working on seeing every one of your movies."

My dad sighed so heavily he sounded as if he might fall over. "All right. I apologize if I jumped to conclusions, Gage."

Chapter 16

Opposition

Gage:

A fire burned in the family room fireplace, the orange flicker giving the illusion of happy-family coziness. I'd started that fire, laid it and everything, which gave me a ridiculous sense of pride. Before I'd met Nova, I'd had no idea how to start and maintain a fire and now I felt like an expert.

Her parents were less impressed. Even the fire and the golden glow of the lamplight couldn't warm them up to me. They were as chilly and unwelcoming as the darkness outside the windows.

I'd never been given such a long string of dirty looks. Nova's dad seemed determined to hate me, which I could easily understand. I'd brought the devil into Jeremy's life and now hers, and I had a long history of partying and womanizing. Did anybody say womanizing anymore?

Whatever. I'd had a lot of women on my arm and in my bed over the past ten years or so. He probably knew that. He'd probably looked me up on the web, checked out my reputation. And it wasn't good.

Jesus, I'd once been proud of all the women I'd had. Now I wanted to hang my head like a whipped dog over the things I'd done before I met Nova. How fucked up was that?

No. It wasn't fucked up. She was the best thing to ever happen to me, full stop. Only I hadn't adjusted my thinking, my self-image yet. Part of me still pictured myself as the party animal who went home with a different woman every night.

That had been an empty life, one I had no intention of taking up again. I'd known it was empty at the time I'd been living it, but I hadn't seen any alternative. Dr. Ray Pennyman didn't know that, however, and I couldn't explain it to him in a way he could understand.

We sat in the family room drinking coffee Nova made, while her dad glared at me over his mug. At one time, I would've found this highly amusing. At one time, I wouldn't have given half a shit what he thought of me, but that time was over. He was Nova's dad, and for her sake I wanted him to like me.

I'd hoped having them over would convince him I wasn't the Big Bad Wolf preparing to gobble his daughter alive. Now that didn't seem possible. Maybe I could salvage something, though, get him to understand I wasn't the enemy.

Good thing he didn't know about The Deal. Then he'd have a real, concrete reason to despise me, instead of a bunch of unfounded suspicions.

Nova brought the last mug of coffee out and settled in beside me, snuggling up against me in what I figured was a gesture of solidarity. I wanted to put my arm around her. Kiss her. But that would most likely set off her dad again, so I just took her hand and laced my fingers through hers.

"I saw your last movie, Gage," Mrs. Pennyman said with a bright smile. Was she putting it on for the sake of peace? I couldn't tell.

"I hope you enjoyed it," I said.

"Oh, yes. You're very talented."

Nova elbowed me. "See? I told you so."

Oh, Christ. Here we go again.

"What are you talking about?" her mom said, looking from her to me and back again.

"He thinks he's not a good actor. He thinks he's a fraud."

"Nova," I whispered as my face burned. "Cut it out."

"It's true. You've told me that more than once," she said.

Her mom tilted her head. "Really? You don't think you're any good?"

I shifted. Her husband watched me intently, like a predator looking for a weak spot.

"I think I've been really lucky, that's all."

Her dad snorted. I stared at him from across the family room. So far I'd cut him a lot of slack because of Nova, but he was starting to piss me off. Did I confront him or let him run roughshod over me in my own house?

"Ray," Mrs. Pennyman muttered under her breath. "You promised."

"Well, at least you acknowledge you don't deserve your fame," Ray said.

I pursed my lips. "Look, Dr. Pennyman, I'm trying to be nice for Nova's sake, but I'm starting to lose my cool here. You're picking a fight with me and I don't know why."

"I thought I was pretty clear about why."

"You don't think I'm good enough for her."

"No, I don't." He said it flatly, looking right into my eyes.

"That's unfortunate. I think it's up to Nova to make that decision," I said.

"Exactly." Nova leaned forward. "Dad, you're breaking something here. Is that really what you want?"

Her dad frowned. "He's that important to you?"

That was the kicker, wasn't it? And her dad was right. I wasn't worth it. I shouldn't come between a beautiful girl like Nova and her family.

"Yes." She squeezed my hand. "I love him."

Something in my chest and throat seemed to swell until I found it hard to swallow. She loved me. Still. After I'd left her, after I'd endangered her, after I'd barged back into her life, she loved me.

The reciprocal words hovered on my tongue. I wanted to say them so badly, almost more than I wanted to keep my soul.

My gaze wandered to the windows on either side of the fireplace. I don't know why I looked in that direction; it was just one of those random things. And I saw him.

A dark-haired man in a fitted black suit. He was reflected in the window, as if he stood inside the room. Except no-one was there, only us humans. Nova didn't seem to notice his reflection.

My heart banged against my ribs as I stared at the reflection and tried to keep my reaction from showing. I didn't want to alarm her parents. The suit-wearing man's dark eyes met mine. He could see me. He knew I was looking at him.

He smiled.

Oh, God. I kept my poker face, but part of me shriveled up at the sight of that smile. Because now I couldn't say I love you back to Nova. I couldn't do that to her, not with *him* watching and listening. I had no idea whether he was Lucifer himself or merely a deputy, but either way I didn't want news of my feelings for her to get to the Prince of Hell.

At the same time, I didn't want her to lose face in front of her parents, didn't want to humiliate her like that, let alone disappoint her.

I leaned over and kissed her cheek, my heart full and warm and hurting. "You are so sweet."

"You don't have to say it back," she said, giving me a quick sideways glance. "That's not the point."

It was for her parents. I could see it in the disapproving looks they were both giving me. They clearly thought I was taking advantage of her. Using her.

"I love him," she repeated. "I'm staying with him, no matter what anyone else says. So I guess it's up to you guys whether you can deal or not."

"I don't think I can," her dad said with a quick shake of his head. "I'm sorry. I just can't approve of what you're doing here. You haven't known each other more than a few weeks, but you're moving in together? It doesn't make any sense."

"It does to us," Nova said.

"I really think you're making a huge mistake here."

"I hear what you're saying, Dad, but you can't change my mind."

"Then I guess there's nothing more to say to each other." He stood. "Come on, Louise."

Nova sighed heavily. She watched as her dad left the room. Her mom walked over to us and patted each of us on the shoulder.

"He'll come around," she said softly. "Give him a little time."

Nova grabbed her mom's hand. "Thanks, Mom."

"It's okay, honey. Really, it is." She smiled at me, her eyes both warm and sad. "Gage, I'm so glad I got to meet you. I'm sure we'll see each other soon."

"I'm glad you could come over," I said. "Let me show you out."

"Oh, no, don't bother. We'll see ourselves out. I wouldn't want Ray to start a fistfight." She winked at me.

"No, we wouldn't want that." The last thing I needed was to beat up Nova's dad.

Her mom disappeared into the hallway. Nova looked at me with a conspiratorial smile.

"What?" I couldn't understand what she was smiling about.

"You won over my mom. This is the first time she's been supportive of my choices."

"Really?" I frowned. "I wonder why?"

"It's your irresistible charm," she said.

Suddenly, my inability to express what she really meant to me became too much to bear. I had to keep it to myself. But I had to let her know the truth. It was an impossible situation all around.

I wrapped my arms around her and hauled her into my lap. Buried my face in her fragrant hair. "Babe, I wish I could tell you everything I'm feeling right now."

She tucked her face in against my neck. "Why can't you?"

"Because of The Deal." Because he was still there, watching us, that smile fixed on his face. *I love you. I love you. I love you.*

"It's all right." She kissed my neck.

I closed my eyes. "No, it isn't. Nothing about this is right."

"Gage, they're just words." One small hand moved up to my jaw and pressed on my face, turning me toward her.

She captured my mouth with hers and I surrendered. The wet heat of her mouth felt like sanctuary, like home, like paradise. She was my home, my safe place. But she was also mine to protect.

I pulled back. "Not now," I whispered.

"Why not?"

"He's here." My arms tightened around her. "No, don't look. I'm hoping he can't hear me."

"Is he looking through the window?" she whispered back.

I swallowed. "I can see him reflected in the window. Like he's standing in the middle of the room."

She gave a little start, then clung to me. "Oh, God. How did he get in here? Why can't we see him?"

"Who knows?"

"Will he attack us?"

"I don't know, babe." I forced myself to loosen my grip on her a little. If I held her any tighter, I'd cut off her air.

All I wanted was for Nova to be safe. Yet he'd managed to invade my home—our home—and I had no idea whether I could make good on my promise to protect her. I knew how to fight, but not how to battle an evil spirit. You can't put a demon into a head lock.

I glanced up and his reflection was gone. A quick visual inspection of the room turned up nothing.

"I think he's gone," I said.

She raised her head and looked around. "Well, I don't see him anyway. What a creep."

I laughed a little. "Yeah, no kidding." Then I sobered, because nothing about this was funny. "Your dad's right about me."

"No, he isn't."

"Yeah, Nova, he is. I'm not good for you. If I thought it would help, I'd send you far away from me."

"You realize you can't order me around, right?" she said, frowning sternly at me.

"Just let me have my male fantasy, will you?"

Nova grinned. "Oh, is that what it is?"

We were pretending, whistling in the dark, making believe that because we could tease and laugh, we were safe. Even while the devil lurked in the corners, waiting for a chance to ruin us.

***

Nova:

I was in love with the kitchen. I'd never been in love with a room before, but this was the real thing. The quality of the cabinets and hardware, the flooring, the appliances—it was all topnotch, and that made cooking a lot more fun. Besides, the white cabinets and tons of light from all the lamps made it a cheerful place to work.

Gage and I had come to a compromise on my safety issues. I had my truck and I went to work alone. But I didn't go anywhere else and came straight home, and if I wanted to go out again I took him with me.

If he'd started quizzing me on my whereabouts or telling me where I could and couldn't go when I wasn't with him, I would have started to worry. But he didn't. Besides, this situation wasn't exactly normal so I couldn't blame him for being a bit over-protective.

The only problem was his identity. We still had to go to certain lengths to prevent people from figuring out who he was.

The last few days had had an eye-of-the-storm quality about them. Too quiet, as if at any moment the shit would hit the fan. Skylar had spilled her news all over Facebook, Twitter, Instagram, Vine, you name it. Every social media outlet. We'd gotten calls, but no-one had shown up at the house yet.

We'd spent most of our spare time at the house or in the yard, just because it felt safe. Private.

I finished making dinner for the evening, put the chicken in the oven to roast. Then I washed my hands and wandered over to the stairs to go up to the bedroom and join Gage for a nap. But the sound of guitar strings coming from the office stopped me in the hallway.

Gage was playing again. I paused to listen. That guitar he'd found in L.A. had an oddly beautiful quality to it that I couldn't really find words to describe. I mean, I like guitar music in general. But this particular instrument—I couldn't quite decide what it was about the sounds that came out of it, just that they felt more powerful, more moving, than any other guitar music I'd ever heard.

He kept stopping, though. He'd play a bar or two, then stop for a minute. Then he'd play the same bar, but with a minor variation. I inched closer to the open door to see what he was doing without being found out for spying.

He sat on the office couch, his head bent over his guitar. Then he reached over the instrument to scribble something on a pad of paper resting on the coffee table. Wow, hold on. Was he composing a song?

I didn't know he did that.

Taking up the guitar again, he began to sing.

You think I've forgotten you
Your sweet face
The way you kissed me and said you loved me
You think I've forgotten you
But I will never forget

I know I'm not good enough for you
November Daye, you deserve better than me

At the end of the piece, he stopped again to make more notes on his paper. I grasped the doorjamb. The song was about me. November Daye was my full name. No-one had ever written a song about me before.

I wanted to run into the room and throw my arms around him and thank him. But something told me he wasn't ready to let me hear the song yet. I didn't want to ruin it for him or embarrass him, so I tiptoed away before he realized I was there.

Chapter 17

Paparazzi

Nova:

In the winter in Avery's Crossing, the sky is usually so gray that you can't really see the shadows. That makes it hard to know what time of day it is without looking at a clock. This day was no different, the sky a uniform steel tone that gave no hint of the time—four in the afternoon—but which strongly suggested rain.

Imagine that. Rain in the Willamette Valley in the winter. Huh.

The house that Gage was buying felt so cozy and bright inside, though, that the gray weather didn't bother me like it normally did. Even the pale gray paint on the walls didn't seem gloomy, just gentle.

With the security team off duty, the house was even quieter than usual. Gage and I were completely alone at the moment. My parents had gone back to Portland because they couldn't neglect their practices. But, a week later, they were down here again, staying at the Holiday Inn despite the dust-up we'd had over my decision to stay with Gage. They hadn't come back to the house, though.

Were they punishing me—or trying to, anyway—by keeping their distance? I couldn't be sure. One thing I was sure of, though. No matter what they did, I wasn't leaving Gage.

The room-sized closet in the master bedroom was still mostly empty, although I'd managed to sneak my clothes over. My pitiful wardrobe did little to fill up all that space, but that wasn't important. The mission of the moment was to get dressed in something work appropriate and get downtown before I was so late my boss fired me.

I pulled out some leggings and a long tunic. Today was my first full shift at The Unique Boutique in quite a while. I didn't want to disappoint my boss, and besides I needed the money.

"How old are you?" Gage said from his post on the island bench. He liked to watch me dress.

"Twenty-two. Why?"

"It occurred to me when your mom called the other day that I didn't know." He pulled me onto his lap, clothes and all. "I was worried you were underage."

"Not too worried, if you didn't say anything."

He nibbled on the side of my neck. "I trust you. But I wanted to be sure."

His erection pushed erotically against my ass. I reached around and cupped the back of his head with my hand.

"I have to go to work." I bit back a sigh as he nuzzled me. "We can't do this right now."

"I hate your job."

I laughed. "Too bad. I need it."

"No, you don't. You have me."

"You're not my job and I won't be a kept woman."

His arms tightened around me. "You're not a kept woman, for chrissake."

"I would be if I didn't work." I pushed my hands backward against his chest. "Now let me go so I'm not late."

He growled playfully. "Fine. Abandon me. I'll be all right."

I jumped off his lap. "I know you will. You can finish that song you've been working on."

His lips curled at the corners and his eyes crinkled up. "How did you know?"

"I have my ways," I said in a mysterious tone, pulling up my leggings.

"You listened in?"

I yanked the tunic over my head. "Just—no, not really. Only when I walked past the door of the office."

"How often did you walk past the door?"

I poked my head out of the tunic's neck hole. "Uh...do I have to answer that question?"

"That is an answer."

I was so not addressing the fact I'd been eavesdropping on his music sessions.

"It sounds beautiful," I said. "What you have so far."

He smiled up at me, that brain-melting, life-changing smile that nearly killed me every time I saw it. "You'll be the first to hear it when it's done."

"Promise?"

"Yep. I promise."

I leaned down and brushed a kiss over his lips. "Okay. I gotta run."

I stuck my feet into a pair of flats and dashed out of the bedroom, admiring the gorgeous upstairs hall as I made for the stairs. Every day I took a few seconds here and there to appreciate the incredible house I currently occupied. It wouldn't last forever and I wanted to savor the experience.

Grabbing my purse off the table in the foyer, I ran for the door.

"Have a good day," Gage called from upstairs.

"Thanks, babe!" I opened the door.

Cameras flashed in my face. Lights went off all around me, from every angle. People, mostly men, crowded around me, yelling.

"Look this way, Nova!"

"Nova! Over here!"

"Are you and Gage getting married?"

I flung an arm up, as if that gesture would hold them at bay. My truck sat in the driveway, well beyond the ring of aggressive reporters or paparazzi or whoever these people were. I should have put it in the garage so I could get to it without going outside. Why hadn't I put it in the garage?

"Excuse me," I said, all too polite. "I have to go now."

I tried to move forward, but the men refused to budge. They only stuck their cameras in my face again, yelling more questions and admonishments at me. Was I pregnant? How long had I been with Gage? Had Gage and I ever had a threesome?

Much of the shouting was lost on me. I couldn't hear all the individual questions over the clamor. It sounded like nothing more than a wall of noise.

I stared at the man directly in front of me. He had muddy hazel eyes and thinning blond hair. I took a step toward him. He backed up, so I kept going forward. The others continued to crowd around, following me as I made painfully slow progress toward the steps, some of them coming around to my back. Cutting me off from the house.

I reached the stairs. My gaze snapped to my truck, just a few yards away. Safety, if I could get to it.

A man stood next to the passenger door. He looked familiar—tall, black-haired, wearing a fitted black suit. He smoked a cigarette. Although the cigarette put off clouds of sweet-smelling smoke, I could see his eyes through the haze, watching me.

My gut chilled as I recognized him. I'd seen him before, that day when I'd gotten coffee at the M.U. with Skylar and again that other night in the back yard here at the house. He'd been staring at me then, too.

Someone behind me bumped into me, shoving me down the steps. I lurched forward, stumbling down the first stair and toward the man who'd done all the backing up. He backed up again, a jump backward, and I tumbled forward, landing on my hands and knees on the rough flagstone paving.

The cameras flashed. The men yelled. I bent my head, trying to get my breath back, trying to get my feet under me.

"Nova!" Gage's enraged shout came from behind us.

I looked over my shoulder, but the paparazzi blocked my view. All I could see was the top floor of the house, looming over us, and the intent faces of the men as they aimed their cameras at me.

"Get the fuck out of my way," Gage snarled.

The camera men parted, revealing a furious Gage. They kept snapping shots as he bent over me and took my trembling body in his arms. He drew me to my feet and put his arms around me, pulling me in against his chest.

"What the fuck is the matter with you?" he shouted at the men. "She fell. She could be hurt and all you can do is keep shooting?"

He turned, with me still in the circle of his arms, and helped me up the stairs as the vultures continued taking pictures. They fell away from him, though, as he brought me back to the house.

At the door, he turned back to the crowd. "This is private property. You are trespassing. Get the fuck off my land before I call the sheriff." He bent his head to me. "Come on, baby."

With one arm around me, he used his free hand to open the door. We shuffled inside and he shut the door, locking and bolting it against the madness outside. Then he drew me against his body once more, locking his arms tightly around me.

"Are you okay?" he said. "Did they hurt you?"

"I—I don't know. I d-don't know."

"Okay. It's okay, Nova. Let's go in the family room and have a look."

I took a couple of steps in that direction and my knees buckled. Gage swept me up and carried me. I didn't even protest, passively allowing him to carry me as if I were a child.

He sat down on the couch with me, holding me on his lap, the heat and strength of him giving me comfort. "You're not going to work today."

"N-no. I guess not." I tried to laugh, but it came out sounding all wrong. "Thank you for saving me."

"Anytime. I wish I'd gotten there sooner."

"How did you know I needed you?"

He kissed the crown of my head. "I wanted to watch you leave. Dumb, huh?"

"No, it isn't. I'm glad you did." I rested my head against his shoulder. "I was really scared."

"God, I'm so sorry." He tightened his grip on me and laid his cheek against my head. "I never wanted anything like that to happen to you. That's the last time I give the security guys all the same day off."

"I'll be all right in a few minutes."

"Your leggings are torn," he said, beginning to sound agitated again. "You're bleeding."

I looked down. Bloody, scraped knees showed through the rents in my black leggings. I hadn't even felt it until he mentioned it, but as I looked at them they began to sting.

"It hurts a little." I held up my palms. They were scraped, too.

"God damn it," he growled. "Those bastards. They're not supposed to come onto private property."

"How did they find out where you are?"

"Where we are." He kissed the top of my head. "And I don't know. They could have bribed people. Followed us. I don't know."

That reminded me of the man with the cigarette.

"One of them," I said. "I've seen him before. I recognized him."

"When was that?"

"A few weeks ago. It was before you came back. I was out with Skylar, at the Memorial Union on campus, having coffee. This guy was watching me and it kind of gave me the creeps. And then I saw him again in the back yard. Remember when I was hiding in the tub?"

Gage frowned as he gazed down at me. "That's weird. Why would he have followed you to the coffee shop if we weren't together yet? Nobody knew about Subalpine. I mean nobody. Cindy kept it totally quiet."

"I don't know. But he was dressed the same way all three times. A black suit. And he smoked these freaky cigarettes that smell weird."

His face took on that still expression I'd learned meant he was upset. "Dark eyes?"

"Yeah. How did you know?"

"The cigarette made a lot of smoke? Like an unnatural amount?"

"Yes." I twisted my body toward him. "You know that guy?"

"No. But I saw him once, too. In L.A."

"What?" I didn't understand.

"It was when I visited one of those occult stores. I came out and saw him watching me." Gage's big body shuddered. "Plus he was the guy I saw reflected in the window downstairs. I don't think he's human."

"Not human? Then what—oh, my god. The Deal." In the excitement and fear of the paparazzi attack, I'd completely forgotten our supernatural problems.

"Yeah. The Deal." His nostrils flared. "I want you to call that woman. What was her name?"

"You mean Marie?"

"That's the one. Call her. Have her come over here as soon as possible."

I nodded, still shaky. "Okay. I'll do that."

"First let's get you cleaned up."

"Gage, you don't have to baby me so much. I can doctor my own skinned knee."

He took my face in his hands, his gaze intent, eyes narrowed, brows drawn down. "I need to take care of you. This happened to you because of me, and that's not right. I hate that I've brought pain and fear into your life."

I placed my hands over his. "It isn't your fault."

"Yes, it is." His blue eyes were so solemn they almost made me want to cry. "I knew what I would bring down on you, and I came to you anyway. I should never have done that."

He was scaring me. Would he walk away from me in a misguided attempt to protect me again?

"Please don't talk like that. I'm glad you came. I want you in my life."

He shook his head. "Nova—"

"Don't you dare." I put a finger over his lips. "Don't say we can't be together. I don't want to hear that."

"I'm not good for you." His lips felt soft and warm as they moved under my finger.

"Yes, you are." I removed my finger and replaced it with my mouth.

He opened for me instantly. I tasted him with a sweep of my tongue and he sighed against my mouth. My hand strayed to the side of his jaw, my thumb rubbing against the stubble there. His fingers delved into my hair, holding me in place for the kiss. As if I would ever try to get away.

I looped an arm around his shoulders. One of his hands left my skull to slide down my back to my ass. He gave me a squeeze.

Then he moaned and pulled back. "Babe, we need to get you cleaned up."

"No." I tried to pull him down for more kissing.

"Yeah. I want to make sure you're okay."

"I'm fine."

"You could get an infection. Come on." He stood up again, lifting me as he did it. Damn, he was strong, and that was a major turn-on.

"This reminds me of when we were up at the cabin," I said, biting his ear lobe.

"No woodsmoke."

"You're bossing me around and making me do things I don't want to do."

He laughed darkly. "Now you're sounding kinky. Maybe I won't doctor your knee after all."

I smacked him lightly on the shoulder. "Gage!"

"What?"

Those big eyes of his could look remarkably innocent at times. Except they weren't. He wasn't. I wondered how much kinky sex he'd had, and what kind. Not that I knew anything about that. Plus I really didn't like thinking of him with other women, even if he was exclusive with me now.

Was he exclusive with me? We hadn't actually talked about that.

He came to the staircase. I glanced up at the long flight of stairs and then back at him.

"You're not carrying me up that."

Gage took the first stair. "Yeah, I am."

"I'm too heavy."

He just laughed.

Chapter 18
Call For Help

Nova:

Gage and I sat in the sparsely-furnished office, which was where he'd been keeping his guitar and working on his music. I hadn't spent much time in this room, but he'd wanted to play while I made the call and I wanted to be with him. The room featured plantation shutters, the vanes turned up and pointing at the ceiling for privacy, a modern glass and steel desk, a sofa covered in persimmon-colored chenille that matched the one in the family room, and a fluffy white flokati rug on the floor. Plus Gage's guitar.

I was pretty sure he planned on making this the music room.

My palms felt slick as I sat at the desk and dug my smart phone out of my bag. Nerves. They were killing me. I'm not usually shy about talking on the phone—or in person—but calling Marie gave me the heebie-jeebies.

I dialed her number, glancing at Gage for support. He didn't even notice, since his head was bent over his guitar as he picked out a soft melody. I didn't recognize it, but I did know it wasn't the one he'd been recently working on.

My guy wrote songs. How cool is that?

Marie's phone rang. My hand tensed as I waited for her to pick up. Although she'd offered to help me, this felt so awkward and strained and I hadn't even spoken to her yet. I'd never called a stranger to ask for help before.

"Hello?" It was a deep, male voice on the other end.

"Oh. Uh, is Marie there?" I stammered.

"Who's calling?"

"Uh, Nova? My name is Nova. Marie told me I could call her."

"You're that girl from the bookstore, right?"

"Yeah," I said, relieved.

"I'm Brad, Marie's husband. I'll go get her."

I should have calmed down at that, but my palms felt even sweatier than before. Should I tell Marie the true nature of our problem or let her figure it out on her own? I supposed it would be a test of sorts, to see if she was the real deal. If she spotted the devil's fingerprints on me and Gage, she would definitely earn much greater trust from us.

"Nova?" Marie's voice made me jump.

"Yeah. This is Nova."

"Are you all right?"

I took a deep breath. "Not exactly, no. Something more happened."

"It's getting worse, isn't it?" Marie said, sounding concerned.

"Yeah. I think it is."

"Do you want to talk about it over the phone or would you rather do this in person?"

"I think in person would be better," I said, sending Gage another glance, only to find him as deeply immersed in his music as before. "Yeah. I think you should see both of us."

"Both of you?" Marie said. "Your boyfriend is there, huh?"

Okay, that was weird. How had she known? Oh, yeah, she probably had a Twitter account or Facebook or something, and had seen all the gossip about me.

"Yeah, he's with me," I said. "We'd both like to talk to you, if that's okay."

"Sure it is. Brad and I were just about to sit down to dinner."

"Oh," I said, disappointed. For some reason, I'd pictured her jumping right in her car and racing over here to save us. "I'm sorry. I didn't mean to disturb your dinner time."

"No, no, that's not what I meant. How about we box up the food and take it to your place and we'll all eat together?"

"Uh…" I'd never had anyone make an offer like that to me. "Are you sure? It seems like an awful lot of trouble for you."

"It's no trouble. I'll get the boys to do all the work." She laughed.

"Do you have sons?" Was she planning to bring them to our house?

"In a sense. I meant Brad and our foster son, Max. He's here now, and he's very knowledgeable about occult goings-on. Would you mind if I brought the men over?"

"No, not if they can help." We'd have an entire team working for us. This could be a good thing.

"We'll be over as soon as possible."

I gave her the address and cut the connection. Gage looked up from his guitar, continuing to strum a soft chord progression as he smiled at me.

"She's coming over here?"

"Yeah. She's bringing her husband and their foster son."

"Oh." He made a thoughtful face. "I guess that's all right."

"It sounds like they're all into occult stuff, so maybe they'll be able to give extra help."

"Then it's a good thing they're coming, because we can use all the help we can get." He set the guitar aside.

"No kidding." I walked over to him and he put his arms around my waist, pressing his face against my belly. I cradled his head, burying my fingers in his soft hair. "I love your playing."

"Thank you." He tilted his face up. "I want to do more of it. Take it more seriously."

"I think that would be great."

"Do you? You're not just saying that?"

"No, I'm not just saying that. You're really talented."

God, he had the most stunning eyes. I could stare at them forever and not get bored. They were so damn blue, and so big, so long-lashed. Women would kill to have eyes like that. I traced the curve of one dark eyebrow with my forefinger before laying my palm against the side of his face. He turned into my caress, his eyes closing.

My heart felt too big for my chest. I wanted to tell him how I felt about him, but he probably wouldn't want to hear it. And if he didn't feel the same way, it would make things uncomfortable between us. So I said nothing, merely bending down and kissing his forehead as a substitute for words.

"What are we doing for dinner?" he said.

"Oh, yeah, I forgot. Marie and company are bringing food over."

"What?" His eyes popped open.

"She said they were just about to eat and that she and the boys could bring the food over here if I wanted. So I said yes."

"That's amazingly generous of her."

"That's what I thought."

"I wonder how far away they are," he said, rubbing his face against me. "Do we have time for a quickie?"

"Do you know how to do a quickie?" I teased.

He grinned lasciviously at me. "I'm pretty sure I can figure it out."

His hands slipped up beneath the hem of my tunic, which in the absence of the leggings had become an extremely short dress. I needed to change.

Gage clasped my ass in his big hands, squeezing as his mouth traveled slowly across my breasts. He paused at one nipple, biting softly through my clothing. I gasped.

He did it again, eliciting a loud moan from me.

"Take this off." His voice sounded hoarse as he pushed my tunic up my body.

I grabbed the hem and hauled it over my head. "Is that better?"

"Much." He reached up and flicked open the center clasp of my bra, releasing my breasts. His calloused hands cupped me, warm and strong on my soft flesh.

"Mmm," I said, arching into his touch.

He lifted one breast and took my nipple into his mouth, suckling powerfully. I groaned and clutched his head to me as sharp spears of arousal shot from my breast to my sex. My core ached with yearning.

His free hand yanked my panties down around my hips, then farther south until he'd gotten them all the way to my knees. He still had his mouth on me. I stood on my right foot and hooked my toe in my panties, hauling them down to my left ankle until I'd freed my left foot.

"Better," he muttered against my breast.

He returned to suckling me, but his hand slid between my legs. Then he grabbed my left thigh, bending my knee and settling it on his leg. This opened me to his touch.

His forefinger traced my folds, sending shocks of delight through my sex. I whimpered.

"So wet," he whispered. "Do you like this, Nova?"

"Yes." I sounded out of breath.

"Do you want more?"

"Yes."

He looked up at me with wicked eyes as his hand paused in its exploration. "Yes, what?"

"Yes, please."

"Like this?" He stroked me along the edges of my core.

"That's good," I whispered, beginning to pant.

"Kiss me."

I leaned forward to obey. His mouth captured mine in a hot, wet invasion that made me moan again. At the same time, his finger plunged inside of me. I gave a sharp cry against his mouth. He made me insane with need. My hands trembled as I tugged at his T-shirt, attempting to get it off him. It didn't want to cooperate.

Instead of helping me, he merely worked his finger harder and faster inside me, pressing on some magical spot in the walls of my sheath. My hands stopped working. All I could do was clutch at him, whimpering and crying as he made me come.

The shock waves of ecstasy died down. I collapsed against him, shuddering.

"God, you are hot," he said roughly. "I want to fuck you hard, Nova."

I moaned. "Yes."

My hands fumbled at his zipper. I got him unzipped and his cock sprang free. No underwear. I stared down at him, surprised, and he gave me a lopsided grin.

"More efficient."

I took him in my hand. He was huge, and I still marveled every time I saw or touched him there at the size and power of him. His cock twitched in my hand. He moaned.

"Sit astride me," he said.

"On the couch?"

"Yeah." He lifted his hips and yanked his jeans down to his muscular thighs. "Go on."

"Okay." I climbed onto his lap.

With my knees on either side of his hips, I guided him to my entrance, sliding his tip against my soaking wet folds.

"God, Nova, just do it. Please."

"I like it when you say please," I whispered. Then I seated him more firmly in my entrance and sank down on top of him, taking him into me to the hilt.

His eyes rolled back in his head as his mouth opened on a long groan. "Fuck, yeah."

"Now what do I do?" I whispered.

His eyes flew open, but he looked lost in pleasure. "Huh?"

I grinned. "What do I do now?"

He stared at me, his eyes going even darker as his hands clasped my ass. "Up and down, baby," he rasped. "Let me show you."

He lifted me up along his shaft, then slammed me back down. I cried out as pleasure and pain shot through me.

"Now you do it," he said. "I'll help."

I rose up, Gage helping me, lifting me, his hips coming up to meet mine. Then pushed myself back down, impaling myself on him. He filled me, stretched me to my limit. I gave a broken groan at the overwhelming sensation of him inside me.

"Nova," he moaned.

His grip on me tightened, fingers digging into my flesh. He worked me hard, up and down on his shaft, staring down at the place where our bodies joined. I leaned my head against him and watched, too, watched his huge cock sliding in and out of my pussy. Something about watching it happen made it ten times hotter than ever, dragging continuous whimpers from my throat. Drawn-out moans issued from Gage, too.

His eyes were wild as he lifted his head and looked up at me. He dragged my head down to his and as our mouths joined, another orgasm crashed through me. I dug my nails into his shoulders, moaning, rocking my hips against his as I shattered inside.

He quivered. His thrusts picked up speed. He groaned and shouted against my mouth. His ejaculate flooded into me, turning me even slicker and wetter.

I held him as he shuddered and panted. Our foreheads rested against each other. Gage stroked his hands up and down my back. He moved his head and pressed a kiss to my right eyelid. Then another to my left. Then he kissed the bridge of my nose, my cheeks, my ear.

"I want you to know," he murmured, "how glad I am that you're here with me."

"I am too."

We exchanged dreamy smiles, our gazes tangling, lingering as we looked at each other. I felt as if I could fall right into him, as if we were merging somehow. The tenderness in his eyes looked like love, even if he didn't say it.

I couldn't think that way, though. The disappointment if I were wrong would be too intense to bear.

The doorbell rang. We both jumped. Then laughed.

"Damn," he groaned. "They're here already?"

"Oh, no," I said, looking down at my naked self. "I haven't even got a whole outfit downstairs."

He withdrew from my body, giving me a last kiss as he did. "Run upstairs and get dressed. I'll get the door."

As I stood up on slightly shaky legs, I remembered my knee was torn up. I glanced down at it. The bandage hadn't moved in spite of all the abuse I'd given it.

"I forgot about your knee," Gage said. He bent forward and kissed me right above the kneecap. "I'm sorry. I should've laid you down."

"It's fine. You're so good I forgot all about it." I grinned at him as I left the room to get ready for our visitors.

Chapter 19
Visitors

Gage:

The office slash music room looked a lot softer in the fuzziness of afterglow, even with visitors standing on our porch and waiting.

Nova grabbed up her tunic. "Don't tell them about the devil. I want to see if Marie can figure it out on her own."

She scampered out of the room. I watched her cute, naked ass jiggling as she dashed for the door and wished we could go for round two instead of dealing with our devil issues. But duty called. If this Marie lady was as knowledgeable as she seemed, we might be able to find a way out of our problem.

I wiped myself off with a tissue and tucked myself back into my jeans, hoping no-one would notice the smell of sex clinging to my body. Then I padded to the front door in my bare feet and opened it to find three people standing on my front porch.

The overhead lamp hanging from the porch ceiling cast cool, white light across their faces and long, gray shadows behind them. The shadows crossed the floorboards, blended into the darkness of the night, and disappeared.

Two of the visitors were men, one tall and middle-aged with brown hair, the other also tall but young, about my age. His nearly black hair and blue eyes, combined with striking features, could have won him a career in show business. The woman accompanying them had long, dark hair worn in a single braid over one shoulder. All three of them carried a box or bag, and all three stared at me, their faces uniformly incredulous.

"You're Gage Dalton, aren't you?" the younger dude said.

"Yep. And you are?"

"Max Kincaid." He stuck out a hand and we shook.

The woman with them smiled at me. "I'm Marie. Nova called me and asked me to come over."

"Yes. Thank you for coming so quickly." If only they could have gotten here a few minutes later. "Come on in."

"Is Nova here?" Marie said, looking around curiously as she entered the foyer.

"She'll be down in a couple of minutes. The kitchen is this way."

I led them to the breakfast room, a much cozier place for eating than the luxe formal dining area.

"I had no idea you were Nova's boyfriend," Marie said, putting the bag she carried on the table.

"We assumed you'd seen the gossip all over Twitter and Facebook," I said.

"Marie doesn't pay much attention to gossip." The older guy set his box on the counter and stuck out his hand. "I'm Brad, Marie's husband."

"Gage Dalton," I said.

"I know." He grinned at me. "You're famous."

I pretended to be shocked. "No way. Really?"

Everyone laughed, but it didn't sound forced. So far they seemed like some of the most relaxed, natural people I'd ever met, especially considering they already knew who I was. They didn't seem to care much about my A-list status.

"Hi, Marie," Nova said softly. She now wore a fresh pair of leggings, ballet flats, and a long waffle-weave tunic in a soft blue. Not a glamorous outfit, but to me she looked like the sexiest woman alive. What I felt for her wasn't safe—for Nova—but I couldn't seem to help myself. I fell for her all over again every time I looked at her.

She glanced at Max, her gaze lingering on his features. I tensed at the sight of her checking out another dude. Did I have competition? If Max made a move for her, I was going to kill him, helper or not.

The moment ended almost as soon as it had begun. She moved to me with a smile and slipped her arm around my waist. I stared at Max as I put my arm around her shoulders and tucked her snugly against my side.

Max's mouth curled up. "Too bad Caroline couldn't make it tonight."

"Who's Caroline?" Nova said.

He looked directly at me. "My girlfriend."

Max had a girlfriend. Okay. I could definitely live with that. Unless he was the cheating kind, which he might very well be. I kept my arm around Nova.

She was trustworthy. I believed in her. But this dude was too good-looking and confident for me to write him off completely as a non-threat.

"I hope everybody likes spaghetti and meatballs," Marie said, starting to unpack one of the boxes.

Nova got out dishes and we sat down to what looked like a big enough feast to feed twice as many people as we had. Whoever had cooked this stuff had real talent; it tasted as good as any restaurant Italian I'd ever had.

"Why don't you describe what's been happening, Nova?" Marie said, passing around a basket of garlic bread.

Nova glanced at me. I gave her a subtle nod of encouragement. She still looked uncomfortable, maybe even embarrassed, and I couldn't blame her. Talking about the devil and demons isn't easy to do in this day and age. You always worry people will think you're crazy.

"So, um, I had this feeling I was being watched," Nova said, toying with her pasta. "But I couldn't figure out who was doing it. And I had some strange events, like when my laptop closed my streaming music tab for no apparent reason. But it didn't seem too threatening until the other day when something attacked me in the art building on campus."

Marie's brows rose. "Attacked you? How?"

"It was like an invisible man grabbed me," Nova said, her hand tightening around her fork. Beneath the table, her knee started bouncing, betraying her nervousness.

"That's unusual," Max said.

"Yeah." Marie frowned, looking more concerned than ever. "So what did it do to you?"

"It pushed me against the wall and held me there. Then someone came into the building—this happened on a Saturday, so I was alone when the attack began. Someone came in, I think a professor, and the whatever-it-was let go of me. I left the building and went to the M.U. for a while because I was afraid to be alone."

"I don't blame you," Marie said.

"There's something else. Gage and I have both seen the same man staring at us, but mostly at different times and places. He saw the guy in L.A. and once here. I've seen him three times in Avery's Crossing. One time he was in our back yard."

As Nova talked, the hair on the back of my neck stood on end. That sense of being watched lurked around the edges of my mind and I almost turned around to see if someone might be peering in through the window. I'd been so busy taking care of her that I hadn't bothered trying to find the man in the suit. Was he still here?

"She saw him here at the house today," I added. "And I've seen him here a couple of times myself."

"Is it all right if I do a reading?" Marie said.

Nova cocked her head, looking puzzled. "Another one?"

"It'll only take a minute or two. I'll scan you, your energy so to speak, and see what I can pick up, just like I did in the bookstore. I can probably find out more just because we're in a private place. Less interference with the energy."

"Right now?" Nova tapped her plate with the tines of her fork.

"Sure, if it's okay."

Nova glanced at me again. I bumped her knee with mine and smiled at her.

126

"It's up to you," I said.

She took a deep breath. "Okay. Go ahead."

Marie's face went blank. It was like she wasn't fully present anymore, or like she was present to something I couldn't see or detect in any way. She gazed in Nova's direction, but her eyes seemed unfocused and hazy. I wanted to touch Nova, to take her hand or press my leg against hers, yet I couldn't because I wasn't sure how that would affect the reading. Instead, I kept as still as possible and waited.

A furtive glance at Brad and Max told me they were pretty comfortable with this procedure. Both of them remained silent and watchful, but neither looked worried or afraid. Their confidence failed to reassure me, though. My girlfriend's well-being was on the line here.

Marie took a sharp in-breath and her gaze snapped back into focus. She blinked. "The darkness around you is much deeper than I originally thought."

Her pretty face looked troubled, her brows drawn together, her hands tense where they rested on the table top.

"What is it?" Nova said.

"Normally I wouldn't speak of this." Marie exchanged troubled looks with her two men. "We don't usually talk about the—" She bit her lip.

"I think it's best if you just come out and say it," Brad said.

Marie nodded. "All right. The devil. What I see around you is the power of the devil."

Everything in the room seemed to go still for a second. The darkness outside the windows pressed in on the room, and the light pouring from the wrought-iron chandelier over the breakfast table could barely hold it back. Our faces were all cast in harsh shadows, light and darkness fighting for dominance.

Nova grabbed my hand, looking up at me. I expected to see fear in her eyes, but instead there was relief.

"You're not surprised," Max said.

"No." Nova squeezed my hand. "We already knew that part, but we wanted to see if you could detect it. What we really need to know is how to deal with it."

Marie frowned thoughtfully. "Suppose you tell me exactly what's going on. Everything you know."

"It's Gage's story to tell," Nova said.

"This is going to sound crazy," I said.

"You might be surprised." Marie smiled at me in a motherly fashion. At least, I thought it might be motherly; it's not like I'd ever had that from my own mom.

"We've seen and heard a lot of bizarre stuff," Brad said. "I doubt you'll shock us."

"Okay." I took an even deeper breath than Nova had. "My mom sold my soul to the devil."

They stared at me. Every one had that deer in the headlights look.

"When I was ten," I elaborated. "She wanted me to be a big movie star. And she felt like we weren't getting anywhere. So she called up Old Nick and struck a deal—my soul in return for fame and fortune."

"Holy shit," Max said.

"Yeah. Pretty much."

"Well." Brad shook his head. "That's one I haven't heard before."

"I have." Marie exchanged a glance with her husband. "But not directly. A friend of a friend, if you know what I mean."

Did that mean she couldn't help me? Did she know someone who could?

"Tell them the rest." Nova leaned against my arm.

"There's more?" Max raised black eyebrows.

"Yeah. My mom claims that he told her he'd take anyone I care about if for some reason he can't get me directly."

Marie cocked her head. "That doesn't sound right. If he's the devil, what's stopping him from taking you? No offense."

"None taken. And I don't know. I thought it was weird too. In fact, I didn't believe that part at all until my friend Jeremy died of an overdose. I felt something there, when I found him."

"Whoa. Hold on, back up. You found your friend's body?" Marie leaned across the table toward me, as if riveted by my story.

"Yeah. Jeremy Lindstrom. He died of an overdose about six months ago. I found his body when I went to his place."

"I remember that," Max said. "Jesus, that must have been rough."

"Yeah." I dropped my gaze to the table top.

Finding Jeremy had been one of the worst days of my life. I'd tried to help him, but my help had been half-hearted at best, considering I was his partner in crime for so much of the drugging and partying we did. I would have blamed myself anyway for his death, but when I felt that ominous presence in his apartment, my mom's warnings had come back to me full force. The Deal she'd made, using my soul, had killed my best friend.

"I felt this thing in his rooms," I said. "I felt like I was being watched. It scared the hell out of me, frankly, and I don't scare easy."

Marie shuddered. "I don't blame you. I can feel the nastiness now. It's like the memory is bringing it out of you."

I could feel it too, even more strongly now. All the hair on my body seemed to be standing on end at once.

"I'm worried about Nova. He might come after her. No, he already has come after her. When he attacked her in the art building, he mentioned me by name, so I know it's connected to The Deal."

"I still have a problem with this entity," Marie said. "Why would it need to take your friends? Why couldn't it take you? I wonder if it's really the devil at all. Maybe it's some lesser demon messing with you, lying about its identity. They've been known to do that."

"If that's the case," Brad said, "you should be able to protect yourself from it."

"I have a question." Max leaned forward, too, propping his chin on his hand. "How do you know your mom even made this deal? Maybe she just made it up."

"I saw it. I was there when she called him."

Max shook his head. "No offense, bro, but your mom is some piece of work."

"Don't I know."

"My family's fucked up, too, so I know how it is."

That's right. Marie had identified him as her foster son, not her biological son. What had happened to Max?

"Long story," he said, almost as if he'd read my mind. "Let's just say it was so bad I ran away. Marie and Brad got me off the streets."

"I guess I really am lucky," Nova muttered.

"How did you meet Gage?" Marie said. "If you don't mind my asking."

"Not at all." Nova glanced at me with a secret smile. "I was living in a cabin up in Subalpine. Gage fell in the river behind my place and I pulled him out."

"Jeremy," I said.

"Oh, yeah. Jeremy's ghost appeared to me and told me he needed help getting his friend out of the water. When I followed him down to the river, he disappeared."

"So Nova saved your life?" Max said.

"Yep. She did. We spent that big snowstorm back in November together."

"I can see why you're so protective of her," he said.

I wasn't sure how to take that, so I just smiled blandly and said nothing.

Brad rubbed one eyebrow. "Okay, so we have a demon or the devil, plus the ghost of your best friend? And the ghost is protective of you."

"Yeah," I said.

"Do you want to shut out both of them?" he asked.

"No. Just the devil. I wouldn't mind seeing Jeremy again."

"Let's eat," Marie said. "The food is getting cold and we'll all handle this better on full stomachs. I'll give some thought to this and after dinner we'll talk more."

Okay. I could go along with that, although I really wanted answers immediately.

Brad and Max made small talk during the meal, but Marie mostly stayed silent. I could tell she was thinking, really considering everything I'd told her. Normally I wouldn't give much credence to "vibes" or "energy" or whatever New Agers called it, but right now I was getting some very reassuring vibes from these three people. Even Max.

Even if they ended up being unable to help us, the mere fact that they'd listened respectfully had eased the burden a little. Nova and I weren't alone with this impossible situation anymore. On the other hand, we might have just dragged more innocent people into the mess.

Chapter 20
Salt Circles

Nova:

Outside, darkness had long fallen. I could see glimpses of it through cracks in the plantation shutters on the family room windows, not to mention the huge expanse of blackness outside the windows that extended above the shutters. But inside, the air felt warm and lamps glowed. Instrumental guitar music played softly in the background. Max sat on the stone hearth, patiently feeding the fire he'd started and listening to the conversation.

I leaned into Gage's side—we were sitting next to each other on the couch—and he put his arm around me. Now that I was full with yummy food, tucked into Gage's side, with allies all around me, the threat of the demon didn't seem real. Even listening to Marie talk about him seemed fantastical, like a story she was telling us, as if it wasn't part of my life at all.

"We don't know exactly who this demon is," Marie said, "or what he wants, other than to harass you. So I'm going to give you generic protection measures while we work on finding out his identity."

"Okay." Gage nodded.

"Do you believe in God?" Marie said, leaning forward in her club chair.

Gage blinked. "I don't know. I guess so. I mean, if the devil is real then God must be real, too."

"Nothing more concrete than that?" she said, frowning.

"The truth is I never had a lot of faith," Gage said. "I never thought God would be interested in me."

"What about you, Nova?"

I shrugged. "I wasn't raised to be religious, but yeah I believe in God."

"Okay, well, it's important to have what you might call a higher power to call on in these situations. God, Goddess, whatever you name it. Call on the divine because that's the power you need to drive off this spirit."

"Okay." My eyes were wider now. "Should I get myself a cross?"

"If it would help, if you believe it has power, then yes."

I picked at a tiny hole in Gage's shirt. "But if it's only what I believe, doesn't that make it my imagination?"

"No. The power of good, of love, is real," Marie said. "It's only the form your mind gives it that changes. All cultures have some kind of protective, loving deity and that's the power I want you to call on. So if a cross helps you do that, use a cross."

"All right." That would be the first thing on my agenda tomorrow—shop for a cross necklace.

"Another powerful tool is salt," Brad said.

"Yeah." Marie nodded. "Salt protects against all kinds of paranormal entities. If I were you, I'd go to the store and buy the biggest container you can find. If you go to a warehouse store, you can get it in a huge bag." She moved her hands apart to demonstrate just how big the bag was likely to be.

"Whoa," Gage said. "You really think we'll need that much?"

"Yes. Because I want you to make a circle around the entire house, especially doors and windows."

We looked at each other.

"Won't the rain wash it away?" I said.

"Put it inside. Just make a solid circle around your space. That will give you a safe place to retreat to."

"We'll do that as soon as possible," Gage said, sounding determined. I could tell he was going to devote everything he had to this project. "What about circling the bed? Would that help?"

"That would be a great stopgap," she said. "If you have a box of salt in your kitchen. It'll probably take the whole box."

"I think we do," he said.

"We do." I'd used it for cooking.

"You'll sleep easier knowing nothing can get through that circle," she said.

"What if I have to get up to pee?" I said.

"I love how practical you are." Gage smiled down at me.

I flushed. "It's important. 'Cuz otherwise I'll be peeing in the bed, and that's just gross."

Everyone laughed.

"You should be safe enough just going to the bathroom," Marie said. "Make it quick, though. It seems like he's escalating."

Yeah, it sure did.

"Is there anything else we can do?" Gage tightened his grip on me.

"You can smudge," Marie said.

"What's that?"

She reached in her bag and rummaged around for a few seconds. "It's a way to purify a space. Traditional among some Native American peoples."

She pulled a strange-looking object from her bag. It was a grayish bundle of some kind of dried plant, about ten inches long, wrapped in red thread. "This is a smudge stick. It's made of sage. You have to light the end and let it burn. Walk through the whole house, getting the smoke into all the corners of every room. The smoke should drive away anything evil, especially if you pray while you're doing it."

She got up and handed the sage to me.

"Sometimes it doesn't burn all that well and you might have to re-light it. Just keep going until you've smudged the whole house."

"Won't that set off the smoke detectors?" Gage said, peering at the sage.

"Probably." Brad grinned. "But what's more important, protecting your eardrums or keeping this demon thing out?"

"Also, you should have the windows open while you smudge," Marie added. "Otherwise you'll smoke yourselves out too."

"Someone in L.A. sold me some crystals that were supposed to be protective." Gage lifted his hips, reached into his jeans pocket and pulled out a couple chunks of dark-colored crystal. One looked nearly black and the other was a kind of smoky brown-gray.

"Smoky quartz," Marie said, holding out a hand.

"Yeah. And black tourmaline." Gage handed the crystals to her.

"This is good. You should smudge them too before you use them. Then bless them with the power of protection. They'll intensify the effects of everything else you're doing."

"It just doesn't seem like it would be enough," I said. Not to stop the devil.

"I know." Marie gave me a smile that was obviously meant to be reassuring, yet it looked a little ragged to me. Like she wasn't sure how much help she was being at the moment.

"We'll do more investigation to find out exactly what we're dealing with," Brad said. "The sage and salt are just to keep you protected until we can figure out how to actually get rid of this thing."

I took a deep breath. "Okay. That's better than nothing."

"I really wish I could do more for you," Marie said. "Unfortunately, we have a prior commitment this evening. We're already supposed to be there."

"Oh." I looked up at Gage. "Well, we don't want to keep you. Do we?"

"No. We'll be all right."

"Are you sure?" Marie said. "We can cancel. Our friends will understand."

"I don't want to do that to you," I said. "He hasn't really done anything so far. He's probably just trying to spook us."

"Make sure you get that salt circle around the bed," Marie said. "I'll sleep easier too if I know you guys are safe."

"We'll do it right away," Gage said. "If I could, I'd put Nova inside it and keep her there until this crap is all resolved."

I poked him in the ribs. "You would not."

"I so would."

"You need to protect yourself as well," Marie told him. "Don't be macho about this."

"If you want someone to stay with you tonight," Max said, "I volunteer. I can sleep down here on the couch or wherever. Just so there's someone else in the house until you get the whole-house circle done."

Gage stared at him. They'd had some kind of male territorial display going on all evening, at least Gage had. I liked Max, but I could tell Gage didn't trust him and I figured it was because he saw the other guy as a rival. Max was hot, yeah, but he wasn't Gage and I couldn't understand why he thought he had anything to worry about.

I kept quiet. This was something Gage had to work out for himself. If I spoke up, he'd take it the wrong way. I wanted Max to stay, though.

"Look," Max said, "I can tell you don't trust me around Nova. But I'm in love with my girl. I don't want anyone else. I'm only offering out of concern and because they don't really need me at the party. It's more a Marie and Brad thing."

"He's crazy about Caroline," Brad said, winking at me. "And he's been driving us crazy about it since she's been out of town."

Max gave him a dirty look. I smiled to myself.

"I would never cheat on you," I whispered.

"I know." Gage raked his fingers through his hair. "Okay. Thanks, Max. I appreciate it."

"No problem."

"How are you going to get home tomorrow?" Marie said.

"I'll drive him," Gage said.

Chapter 21
Wards

Gage:

The fire Max had started burned bright, casting comforting golden light across the room. It should have cheered me up, but I was too worried about Nova to feel cheerful.

Max sprawled on the orange and gray carpet in front of my fireplace like he owned the house, which I have to admit irritated the fuck out of me. But I owed him, so I kept my mouth shut about it. Besides, he wasn't really doing anything wrong except existing in the same place as the woman I loved. The woman I could never share with another dude, full stop, no negotiation.

I know Max said he was in love with that Caroline chick, but she wasn't here and Nova was. I didn't trust him with her.

"I never met a movie star before," Max said.

"Oh, yeah?" I wasn't being very helpful.

"We don't get too many around here."

He and Nova exchanged a cozy little glance and both laughed.

"Sam Elliot lives somewhere in Oregon," I said, unwilling to reveal his exact location.

"Does he?" Max looked only vaguely interested.

"That's what I hear."

"I love his voice," Nova said.

"So what can you do to help us keep that supernatural fucker out of the house?" I said.

Max raised an eyebrow. "Sam Elliot is supernatural?"

"Funny, Kincaid. You know what I mean."

"You're kinda being a dick," Nova muttered at me.

I knew that and I was fine with it.

Max sat up straight. "I can set temporary wards on the house."

"Well, what's keeping you?"

"I'm sorry about him," Nova said. "He's been under a lot of stress."

"I don't need you making excuses for me," I said. Or growled.

"Gage, dude, I told you I'm not after your girl. I wish Caro was here to set your mind at ease, but she's not. Hey, you wanna see a pic?"

I took a breath and tried to relax. "Okay. Sure."

Max reached into his back pocket and dragged out his smart phone. He flipped through a picture gallery and stopped, smiling with that dumbass infatuated look guys get when they're in love. Jesus, maybe he was telling the truth. There was no other explanation for that puppy-dog look of adoration on his face.

"Here you go." He handed over the phone.

I took it and Nova leaned against my arm to have a look. The shot was of Max and a slim blonde with wildly curly hair. They were looking at each other with just the same look of adoration I'd seen on Max a second before.

"She's really pretty," Nova said.

"Yes, she is."

God, even his voice had that expression in it. I was going to die of sugar overdose. Diabetic coma imminent. Call 911. Did I sound that way when I talked about Nova?

I glanced at her sideways. Yeah, I probably did. Fuck. Couldn't be helped, though.

I handed the phone back to its owner. "Okay, man. Sorry I doubted you. I'm not used to this couple thing."

"It's okay." Max took the phone with a grin. "I get it. I've been there."

"Is she into the magic thing too?" Nova said.

Max shook his head. "Not really. She's a pretty strong psychic and she's picking up a few things here and there just from hanging around me, but her parents don't approve of the occult so it's hard for her."

"That's too bad." Nova glanced at me. "We're having some issues with my folks too. They think Gage is a bad influence."

"Really?" Max looked puzzled. "He's a star, though. What's wrong with that?"

"Everything," I said. "I have a past as a hard partier. Hollywood dissipation and all that."

"Ah. But you don't do that anymore, is that it?"

"Not since I met Nova." I hugged her to me. "Plus Jeremy dying really took the fun out of it."

"It's a good thing," he said. "Drug abuse and demon problems are a bad mixture. Really bad."

I laughed. "No shit."

Max jumped to his feet. "Let's do the wards. Got any olive oil?"

"Sure," Nova said. "I'll get it."

We followed her into the kitchen. She got out the bottle of extra virgin olive oil and a box of regular table salt.

"Will this work?" she said, pushing the EVOO across the soapstone counter to Max.

"Perfect. Plus a small dish or something to pour it in."

I watched him while she went to the cupboard to get the dish. He didn't even check out her very fine ass. So this Caroline chick really did have his loyalty...and that spoke well of him. At one time, I'm sorry to say I would have looked down on him as a pussy-whipped fool but now I respected his attachment. Even if it did make me feel like I needed some strong black coffee to chase the sugar.

Max poured some oil into the little condiment dish Nova got for him. "What prayer would you like to use?" he said.

"The only one I know is the Lord's Prayer," Nova said.

"Okay. That'll work."

"I don't know any prayers." Why didn't I know any prayers? It seemed like a serious oversight now, although I'd never thought I needed them before. Or maybe I'd simply assumed they wouldn't do a guy like me any good.

"Then focus your mind on what you believe about God," Max said. "The best things you can think of."

"That's pretty vague."

"It's okay. Just do what you can. Nova and I will say the words."

I felt pretty damned useless as he held his palm over the oil and spoke the prayer, Nova chiming in. But I tried to picture God.

What did I know about God? I'd spent my life under the shadow of the devil. My mind scanned back over all the books I'd read and the movies I'd seen. The roles I'd played. None of them had much to say about the divine.

Goodness. Mercy. Those words seemed appropriate, so I repeated them over and over in my head. Goodness and mercy. Goodness and mercy.

"Okay, you two keep praying," Max said. "I'll draw the signs on the doors and windows, starting with the front door."

We tagged after him, Nova praying out loud and me just thinking *goodness and mercy* over and over. I'd fooled around with a bit of meditation when I was eighteen but hadn't gotten very far with it. This was the most spiritual work I'd ever done and I felt like an idiot. But it was worth it if it would help.

Max was thorough; I had to give him that. He marked every single window and door in the house, even the cabinet doors. I got tired and kind of bored long before we were done, but he just kept going as if he had endless energy. It wasn't even his house.

I really owed him now. Especially when he went through the master bedroom without even blinking at the mess of women's lingerie Nova had left on the floor.

"That should hold you for a while," he said. "And I'm beat."

"Let's go downstairs and have some coffee," I said.

"Sure."

"Thank you for helping us with this." Nova smiled at him and I didn't feel more than a tiny twinge of jealousy.

"It's nothing." Max waved it off. "I'm glad to help."

"You should play for us, Gage," she said.

That remark set off a whole discussion of music as we walked down the stairs and back to the kitchen for the drinks. Max claimed to play the drums, a fact which I doubted. But I was willing to let him try, since I had a doumbek in the music room with my guitar.

I fetched the instruments and returned to the family room, where Nova had already opened bottles for herself and Max. He saw the drum and his face lit up.

"Thought I'd let you sit in with me," I said, handing it over.

"Cool." He gave the head an experimental roll of his fingers. "This is good, actually. It's always smart to fill up the house with your own positive energy after setting wards. It makes them stronger."

"Does singing in the shower count?" Nova said.

"Yeah, I think so. Anything you can do to put your own positive imprint on the place is good."

How about sex?

I shot Nova a look and decided to keep my mouth shut.

Chapter 22
Whiskey Sour

Gage:

The past two weeks were the happiest I could ever remember. After Max had put up the wards and we'd ringed the whole house with a thick, white line of salt, the paranormal events had completely stopped. Nova and I had the house to ourselves, and when she wasn't at work we spent our time making love in every conceivable position and location.

I was pretty sure this was a snapshot, a preview of heaven. But it couldn't last.

Sometimes I wondered what good all my money and fame were doing me. I couldn't use it to protect Nova. Shit, I couldn't even tell her I loved her, even though every time I looked at her or touched her this giant wave of feeling crashed over me, so strong it sometimes robbed me of speech. And I couldn't tell her that.

I was afraid—terrified, actually—that *he* would hurt her if I did. So I kept my mouth shut, doing everything I could to communicate without words how much she meant to me.

At the moment, she lay naked and face down on the black and white bed while I rubbed warm oil into her back. The sconces on the walls sent interesting patterns of light and shadow across her skin. The oil smelled like sandalwood.

My view at the moment was spectacular. I loved the curves where her tiny waist flared into her hips. I planned to savor that sight, to savor the feeling of her warm skin beneath my hands as I silently told her how much I cared for her.

I just hoped she got the message. Maybe the all-over tongue bath I planned for after the massage would do it.

"Mmm," she moaned as I pushed my fingers in a long glide up her spine. "Where did you learn to do that?"

"I went to school for it."

She laughed into the bedding. "You did not."

"Yeah, I did. It was for a role. I played a massage therapist who does sex work on the side."

"What?" She turned her head to the side and peered up at me with one eye. "You played a gigolo?"

"Yep. *Steamed,* my foray into chick flicks." I performed another slide along the ridges that framed her spine.

"Wow." She moaned again. "Well, you must have been amazing in the movie because you definitely know your stuff."

"I'm inspired right now."

All her moaning, not to mention the sight of her gorgeous body, was making me harder than steel. My cock ached with the need to get inside her. But she'd had a long day on her feet, working at that dowdy little store, and I wanted to make her muscles feel good before I worked on her in other ways.

I put a little more oil on my palms and rubbed it over her scapula.

"God, that feels good," she said.

Yes, it did. I'd never gotten so turned on during a massage before. If I positioned myself just right, I could see the sweet pink lips of her pussy peeking out from between her thighs. Best view in the world.

"You're going to have to show me how to do this," she said, "so I can do you."

"I will. But right now you should just be quiet and let me take care of you." It was the least I could do, considering all the trouble I'd brought into her world.

"You are so not what I expected from a movie star." Her voice sounded muffled because of the bed covers.

"Hush. You're not relaxed enough."

"Shut up, Gage. I want to talk to you."

I smacked her lightly on the ass. "Too bad. I want you to be quiet."

"Ow! Just wait until I get up. Then you'll be sorry."

"Sorry for this?" I gently kneaded her shoulders and she rewarded me with another moan.

Damn. I might not be able to finish the massage after all. My arousal was getting painful.

If we could only stay this way forever, safe with each other, in a private place where we could be real. But the world was going to charge back into our lives again, sooner or later, whether in the form of my career or some supernatural entity. I hated that.

My hands closed over one ass cheek. She was so small, yet so curvy—another thing I loved about her. That pert rear end fit perfectly in my big hands.

I took a moment to stroke her right between her legs. She gasped and gave a little jerk.

"I want you so much." My voice came out husky and rough.

"Then have me." She opened her legs.

Holy shit. I just about came in my jeans.

"Are you sure? I'm not done massaging you yet." As I said this, I continued stroking her between her legs.

"I want you too."

The doorbell rang.

I groaned. "Fuck, no. Not now."

Nova giggled into the bed covers. "You'd better answer it, since I don't have any clothes."

"Let them go away. Where's Cindy? Isn't she supposed to get the door?"

"She's your assistant, not your butler, and she went into town."

"Then let Ted get it." Ted was my main security guy.

Satisfied with my solution, I went back to massaging her, taking a second here and there to tease her pussy.

A minute later, the bell rang again.

"Don't they know how rude they're being?" I said.

"They'll go away eventually." She spread her legs even wider.

I knelt on the bed behind her, right between her thighs. The bell rang a third time.

"Persistent little fuckers, aren't they? What the hell is Ted doing?"

"Maybe he's busy," Nova said. "Go ahead. I'm not going anywhere."

"Shit. All right." I wiped my hands on a towel and adjusted myself in my jeans before I ran grudgingly downstairs.

I didn't bother turning on the foyer light, so the room felt gray and chilly even though the air was warm. The stone floor almost froze the soles of my feet. I caught a whiff of the pizza we'd had for lunch wafting from the nearby kitchen.

At the door, I paused and peered out the peephole, just in case the paparazzi had returned. I froze. Oh, God, no. It was worse than the pap. So much worse.

My mom stood on our porch, an overnight bag slung over her skinny shoulder.

I rested my forehead against the door. Had Cindy given her the address? I needed to have a serious conversation with my assistant.

Unfortunately, I couldn't let my mom stand outside forever. But maybe I could prevent her from moving in with us. She could stay at a hotel until she got bored with life in Avery's Crossing and went home again. Until that happened, I had to keep her from hurting Nova.

The doorbell rang again.

Gritting my teeth, I opened the door. "Mom."

"Hi, Gage!" She swayed slightly, grinning.

Awesome. She was already hammered.

"What are you doing here?"

Her face fell. "I came to see you. My boy. My baby. Aren't you going to let me in?"

"Sure," I said, biting back a sigh. Why not? I could hardly wait to see her and Nova come to blows.

Have I mentioned that my mom and I put the fun in dysfunctional?

I stood back so she could enter. She made a big show of looking around the foyer before she set her bag on the floor.

"It's nice," she said without enthusiasm.

"Not fancy enough for you?"

"Well, it's a little small."

I pressed my lips together, fighting a smile. "Mom, it's just Nova and me and a couple of security guys. We don't need a palace."

"Whatever. Where is this Nova girl, anyway?" She walked away from me, heading for the kitchen.

"She's upstairs. I'll go tell her to come down."

"Is this your kitchen through here?" She pointed.

"Yeah, go ahead and have a look." I bounded up the stairs.

Nova met me in the door to the master bedroom, wrapped in a bathrobe. "Who is it?"

"My mom."

Her mouth dropped open. She looked so adorable it actually cheered me up for a second.

"Your mom?" she said, sounding horrified.

"Yep."

"I'm not dressed. I'm covered in oil."

I grinned as I leaned down to kiss her on her little nose. "Just throw on some jeans and a T-shirt. She won't care."

"Yeah, right." She turned away from me. "Okay, I'll be down in a few minutes."

"Nova, don't worry about impressing her. I don't care what she thinks of you."

She looked over her shoulder at me with a puzzled crease in her brow. "Is that a good thing or a bad thing?"

"It means I care more about what you think than what she thinks."

"Oh." She turned and went on her toes to kiss me. "I love you, Gage."

I love you too.

She disappeared into the bedroom before I had time to stew in my guilt over not saying the words.

Downstairs, my mom was inspecting the kitchen. And by inspecting I mean she was opening each and every cabinet door and drawer to see what was inside.

"Looking for something?" I said.

She raised her head without the slightest indication of guilt or embarrassment. "No. Just seeing what kind of stuff you've got here. You don't have much."

142

"We just moved in." We'd outfitted the place with basic stuff from Target, because it was close by and easy.

"Still." She made one of those dismissive head movements women use to show their disapproval. "It looks cheap."

I clamped down hard on my temper. She'd just gotten here and I already wanted to throw her out.

"Cindy told me this Nova girl is a real redneck."

"She's not a redneck." What the fuck was Cindy's problem, anyway? "And even if she was, it wouldn't matter. I want to be with her. End of story."

"Okay. Okay, don't get all mad at me." She lowered her voice. "It might be better that way anyhow. You know. So you won't get too attached."

Because I couldn't possibly become attached to a country girl? My mom had said some crazy, stupid things, but that one made the top of the list.

"I can't believe you didn't tell me about any of this," she went on, oblivious as usual to my turmoil. "Cindy had to tell me."

"I wasn't ready to share yet."

"You moved out of L.A. and you didn't tell me. I'm your mother."

"Yeah, I know."

She put her hands on her hips. "As long as it's not permanent. You can't work on your career in a Podunk place like this."

"Sure I can. People do it all the time."

She frowned, or tried to anyway. Her eyes narrowed, but her brows didn't move a millimeter. She must have gotten herself botoxed again.

"You can't be serious. You actually want to live in this dump when you could be in L.A.?"

I could smell the alcohol on her breath. She'd probably done nothing but drink since the moment she'd buckled her seatbelt on the plane.

"This is my home now and I don't appreciate you insulting it," I said, moving out of the range of the fumes.

Nova came into the doorway between the hall and the kitchen. I smiled at her and extended a hand.

"Mom, this is Nova Pennyman. Nova, this is my mom, Nancy Dalton."

My mom turned as Nova came toward me. My mom gave her the same kind of once-over Nova's dad had given me, except this was even ruder. Everything about Mom's body language said that Nova came up short, that she wasn't good enough for me.

I walked to my girl and put an arm around her shoulders. Then I kissed her on the crown of her head for emphasis.

"I'm lucky she agreed to move in with me," I said.

"It's so nice to meet you, Mrs. Dalton." Nova extended a hand.

"Likewise." My mom shook without enthusiasm.

Clearly, she'd like nothing better than to hear Nova and I were breaking up. She was doomed to disappointment, though, because I wasn't going to let our crazy parents doom our relationship.

"I wish you'd told us you were coming," Nova said. "We could have gotten a guest room ready."

Oh, no. I should have warned her I didn't want my mom staying with us.

"They're all taken," I put in quickly, before my mom could get any ideas. "Ted and Joe, plus Cindy in the one at the end of the hall."

"Oh, yeah." Nova smiled up at me. "We do have a couple of couches, though."

If I'd known this was going to come up, I would have had somebody haul those puppies away. But there they were, out in plain sight, looking just like the kind of place someone could rest her head for a night or two.

"Maybe Ted could use a couch for a few days," my mom said.

"Then he wouldn't be at his best and I need him to be at his best. I'll put you up at a hotel."

Mom's lips thinned. "I doubt there are any decent ones around here."

"My parents liked the Holiday Inn," Nova said.

"I'm sure they did," Mom replied dismissively. "I'm used to something a little nicer, though."

Nova gave me a speaking look.

"You're the one who chose to come here," I said. "I guess we could put you in Cindy's room. She has a loveseat in there."

It would serve her right if she had to play hostess to my mom, since she was the one who'd informed her where I was.

"I'll bet there aren't any decent restaurants around here either," my mother said.

"Nope," Nova said lightly. "Not a one."

Mom glanced at her, drunken face full of suspicion. Then she looked at me.

"Have you told her?" she said.

"Told me what?" Nova gazed at her with wide-eyed innocence.

"Mom, this isn't the time for that." I pointed at the breakfast area. "Let's sit down and have something to drink."

"Great idea. I'll have a vodka." Mom walked a little unsteadily toward the table.

"We're all out," I said. "How about ginger ale?"

"Ha ha. Very funny. Okay, if you don't have vodka, I'll take a whiskey sour."

"Don't have any of that either."

"Whiskey straight up?"

I shook my head. "No hard liquor in the house, Ma. No beer either."

She peered at me. "Is this a joke?"

"We have coffee," Nova said. "I can make a pot if you'd like."

"The only coffee I drink is Irish." My mom rolled her eyes. "I can't believe you don't have anything to drink around here."

"I told you back in L.A. that I don't drink much anymore."

"Yeah, well, I didn't believe you." She sighed and plopped her butt down on a kitchen chair. "Send Ted or Joe out for something. I can wait a while."

"No. If you want to drink, you'll have to go to a bar."

"Excuse me?" She gave me one of those disappointed mother looks, like I was being a bad boy.

"You heard me. I won't have you getting wasted in my house. You want to do that, you can go to a bar. They even have them here."

She sent Nova a short, sharp glare. "She's making you talk like this to me. Isn't she?"

"Mrs. Dalton, I'm not making Gage do anything."

"Don't take this out on Nova," I said. "I'm not partying anymore and I don't want it in my house."

My mom gaped at me for a minute. Then she shook her head, her eyes filled with confusion. "I feel like I don't even know you anymore."

"You liked me better when I was getting high all the time?"

"Yeah. You were a lot more fun."

Nova gave me an appalled look. I sat down across from my mom.

"I'm sorry I disappoint you by not being an alcoholic," I said.

She rolled her eyes. "Come on, Gage. You know that's not what I mean."

The truth was, I didn't care what she meant. I just wanted her to leave.

"You know, I think I'll sleep on your couch," she announced in a tone that suggested she was doing us a favor. "You need someone around to help you lighten up."

God, no. I exchanged an alarmed glance with Nova.

"You don't have to do that," I said.

"But I want to. What's the matter? You can't stand to have your poor mom around?"

No, as a matter of fact.

"We'd love to have you," Nova said with a sincere-looking smile. She was way too kind for her own good.

"Thank you, honey." Mom gave her a fatuous grin. "I think I like you after all."

Nova smiled back at her, but it looked weak to me. She was fighting to hold on to her composure; I could tell.

"Mom, seriously, I think you'd be happier at a hotel."

"Well, I don't want to stay in a hotel. I want to stay with you. I won't get in your way and there's plenty of room."

I sighed. "Okay. Fine. You can stay on the couch in the music room so you'll have a door you can close."

"Wonderful." She beamed. "You'll see. We're going to have a blast."

Chapter 23

Nancy Dalton

Nova:

The kitchen that normally seemed so generously large, even oversized, now felt way too small, like a pair of shoes that pinch your feet. My beautiful surroundings, the light and bright white cabinets, the sparkling lamps, couldn't cheer up a space that held Gage's mom in it.

I wanted to like Nancy Dalton. I did. She was Gage's mother and I loved him. But this was the person who'd bartered his soul for her own gain, and it pissed me off to sit at the kitchen table with her and pretend to be happy she'd come.

She was bone-thin and wore skinny jeans and platform heels in a shiny nude patent leather. Over that she wore a loose, drapey sweater, the kind that tends to fall off one shoulder. Her lashes were obviously fake and her lips were so shiny I probably could see my reflection in them if I tried.

I could see at a glance that she and Gage were related. She had the same high cheekbones, the same remarkable blue eyes, even the same hair color, although hers was liberally altered with a blonde and caramel color weave. Her similarity to her son did nothing to endear her to me. I wanted to rake her over the coals for what she'd done to him.

Maybe later, when Gage was in another room.

"So, since we don't have any liquor, what would you like to drink?" I said in my best hostess voice.

"Whatever you've got is fine," she said with a careless wave. "If it's not alcoholic, I don't give a damn."

"Okay, then. We do have ginger ale, and also root beer and some off-brand cola Ted brought in. And there's coffee, like I said. And tea."

"Cola," she said.

I got up and went to the fridge. Gage jumped out of his chair, getting to the appliance ahead of me.

"You don't have to wait on us," he said, throwing his arm over the door. "Go sit down."

"Gage—"

"Nova, I don't want you to wait on us."

I stared at him. What the heck was his problem? It's not as if I minded doing it.

"I'm trying to be a good hostess."

"Oh, let her get me a drink," Nancy said.

Gage's lips flattened.

"How about you get one for her and I'll get a couple for us?" I said.

"Fine." He opened the fridge and grabbed a cola.

I didn't know what was going on in his head, but I really wanted Nancy's visit to be as calm and pleasant as possible. So I put on my best fake smile and returned to the table with a ginger ale for me and a cola for him. We were going to be a happy family if it killed us.

Family? No, I needed to stop thinking that way. Gage and I were dating and living together, but we weren't family. He couldn't even tell me he loved me.

Having Nancy in the house was a major intrusion into the fantasy I'd recently been living. I had allowed myself to think that maybe the supernatural bullshit had gone away for good, that maybe our protection methods had actually driven the entity away. Yet now that I sat across from Gage's mom, I couldn't fool myself anymore.

This was the woman who'd started it all, who'd created the nightmarish situation in which we found ourselves. And it wasn't resolved at all. The only thing we'd done was buy ourselves a little time.

Nancy smiled at Gage as he got up and excused himself to go to the bathroom. She watched him walk from the room, a proprietary smugness on her face. Motherly pride I could totally understand, but that expression spoke of something else, something a lot less healthy. It was like she thought of him as a possession or something.

"I'm so proud of him," she said.

"You should be." I gave her a weak smile in return.

She tilted her head, studying me. "You're not like most of the girls Gage has dated. In fact, you're not like any of them."

"Oh?" I really didn't want to hear this.

"He likes the glamorous types." Alcohol fumes wafted heavily from her mouth.

"Mrs. Dalton—"

"You should call me Nancy."

I didn't want to call her Nancy. And why would she tell me that right after she'd insulted me?

"You should get a makeover," she continued. "Get some highlights in your hair, have them teach you how to put on makeup. A new wardrobe, too. Gage would probably pay for it if you asked him."

"That's not why I'm with him."

She pursed her glossy lips. "Yeah, I can see that."

What was going on between us and our parents? It was like they were in a conspiracy together—insult Gage and Nova and try to get them to split up. It wasn't going to work.

"Gage likes me the way I am," I said.

She smirked. "That's probably because he hasn't seen you in context yet."

"In context?"

"Yeah. In L.A., with all the beautiful people around."

I licked my lips. Then I took a sip of ginger ale to buy some time for thought. But there was really nothing to think about, because this level of rudeness was something I couldn't tolerate. She was at least as bad as my father.

"I'm not sure what you're trying to do," I said.

"What is that supposed to mean?"

I tapped my fingertips against the side of my soda can. "Do you not understand how insulting you're being?"

Nancy shrugged. "I'm just trying to prepare you for reality. You're never going to fit in where Gage is from. You can't compete in that environment."

"I don't want to compete." Where the hell was Gage?

"And that's the problem," she said with drunken triumph. "No offense, but I truly don't think you're right for him."

"You sold him to the devil. You're not the best judge of what's right for him."

She stared at me in comical dismay. "He told you about that?"

"Yes, Nancy, he did. I know all about The Deal. And I think if you really cared about him, you would never have done something like that."

"I beg your pardon?" She drew back in theatrical offense.

"You should beg Gage's pardon, not mine. He's the one you hurt."

Her blue eyes narrowed hatefully as she leaned across the table toward me. "You listen here, young lady. I'm his mother. I did what I had to do to help him be successful. It was for his own good."

"It was for your good, not his." I was getting warmed up to my subject and I wanted to see her admit she'd done wrong.

"How dare you? Who do you think you are?" She stood up, a little unsteadily, and glowered down at me.

"Is everything okay in here?" Gage said from the doorway.

Oh, shit. I looked over at him with guilt in my eyes. Fighting with his mom—definitely not cool.

"Mom, what did you say to Nova?" He frowned at her.

"I only gave her a little fashion advice and she insulted me."

He looked at me.

"I disagreed with her decision to make a deal with the devil," I said, trying not to visibly wince.

"Ah." He gave me sympathetic eyes.

"Ah?" Nancy said. "That's all you have to say? Ah?"

"What do you expect? I never wanted it and Nova knows that."

"You're siding with her against me?" Her voice rose in pitch and volume.

Gage shook his head. "Mom, I'm not going to talk about this with you until you're sober."

"Fuck you," she spat.

His eyes widened. "Excuse me?"

"You heard me. I'm your mother and you show me no respect. Who do you think you are? I made you. You'd be nothing if I hadn't done what needed to be done."

Gage rubbed his forehead. "Okay, Mom. Sure. Whatever. Why don't you go into the office and relax?"

"Oh, no. You're not shutting me away in some little cell of a room while you love it up with Miss Redneck here."

He stared at her in blatant confusion. "What are you talking about?"

"She won't last, you know. *He'll* take her. And it serves her right. She just wants to use you, Gage. She wants your money and the glamorous movie star lifestyle."

"Didn't you just tell her she wasn't glamorous enough? Where is all this shit coming from, anyway?"

Nancy raised a shaky hand to brush some over-sprayed hair from her face. "I just—you're going to lose everything. You can't move away from the city. You can't hide out here in bumfuck nowhere. You can't do that, Gage. You need to be in the middle of it all to have the kind of career you want."

Something came over his face, a kind of sadness I'd never seen before. It hurt me to look at it. I wanted to take him in my arms and soothe the pain away, even though I didn't really understand its nature.

"Mom, that's the career *you* want. Not me. Besides, plenty of actors live away from L.A. and they do just fine in the business."

"No. No, they don't. This won't work." She seemed to be unraveling before our eyes.

Gage put an arm around her frail-looking shoulders. "Yes, it will. It'll be okay. You want something to eat? It'll make you feel better."

She looked up at him, her gaze suddenly vague and unsure. "Okay. Yeah, that would be good."

"Okay. Let's make sandwiches." He glanced at me as he shepherded her into the kitchen.

I watched them go, stunned at the weirdness of the episode. Maybe it was just the alcohol, but it seemed like there was something more fundamental in Nancy's nature that was totally screwed up. Like, broken.

I'd wanted, ever since learning about The Deal, to throw it in her face. To tell her exactly what I thought of a woman who would sell her child for any reason and to any buyer, let alone the freaking devil himself. I'd cherished the fantasy of letting her know exactly what a scumbag I thought she was. But now, it seemed...redundant.

Chapter 24

Enough

Nova:

True master suites are wonderful things. You can lock yourself inside and not come out for hours, especially if you have a mini-fridge. Sanctuaries, that's what they are. With a mini-fridge, a bathroom, and a bed, you have everything you need.

They're even better when professionally decorated. When they have tiny accent lamps that cast little pools of warm, glowing light but leave most of the room intimately shadowed and mysterious. There's something really sexy about that.

I curled up on the bed next to Gage and nestled my head against his shoulder, his T-shirt soft against my cheek. "Do you want to be an actor?"

"Yeah, I guess." His voice sounded far away and distracted.

"That's enthusiasm, right there," I said.

"Why do you want to know?"

I draped my arm across his middle. "Something you said to your mom. That it was the career she wanted for you and not what you wanted for yourself."

"I wasn't really talking about acting in general." He wrapped his arms around me. "More about a certain type of acting career. The hot-shot movie star kind of career, where you're constantly putting yourself in the public eye. Where everything you do is calculated for how it'll affect your public persona."

"Is that the kind you've had so far?"

"Yeah, it is. It fucks with your head. After a while, you don't know who you really are anymore. Everything is about the surface, about what other people see in you. At least, that's how it was for me."

"I would hate that."

He gave a soft laugh. "Yeah. Me too."

"You don't have to keep doing it, you know." I tilted my head back to see his face. He was looking down at me. "You could change your direction."

"You think so?" He smiled at me.

"Yeah, I do. If you want to, anyway."

He pushed a strand of hair behind my ear. I loved it when he did that. "I'd probably make less money."

"So? Don't you have enough?"

Blue eyes searched my face. "You think so?"

"It's up to you, Gage. It's your career, your money."

"Yeah, but do I have enough for you?"

I frowned. "I'm not sure what you mean."

"Do I have enough money to make you happy?" He continued to study me, his gaze probing me for information.

What was he really trying to say? Did he mean to imply he wanted to stay with me for the long term? Was he hinting at marriage? Without a declaration of love, that seemed unlikely.

And did he really think I cared about his income? I thought he knew I loved him. The truth was that I was willing to put up with the fame nonsense for his sake, but I'd be happier without it.

"You make me happy, not your money." I cradled his jaw in my hand. "You could quit Hollywood this very instant and I wouldn't mind. But it's your decision. It's about you, not me."

"That's not true. If you're with me, my career affects you. Especially if I go back to L.A."

"But you don't want to go back?"

"No. I don't think I do." He bent his head and pressed his lips gently to mine. "I'd rather commute."

"I want you to be happy," I murmured against his mouth. "I want you to do what makes you feel good. What interests you, what feels meaningful to you." As I said it, I realized I wanted the same thing for myself and was glad all over again that I'd chosen to quit my pre-med program.

"Nova, I—I want to stay with you. I want to be with you."

"I want that too."

He kissed me again. "I know we haven't been together very long. But this is serious for me. I want you to live here with me, even after we solve the devil problem."

"So you didn't ask me to move in just to make sure I wouldn't get hurt?"

"That was a convenient excuse, but no." He combed his fingers through my hair, his eyes fixed on mine. "It's so strange. In some ways, I feel like I've known you forever. I feel like you can see parts of me, parts of my soul, that are invisible to everyone else."

"I feel that way about you too."

"You do?"

I smiled. "Yeah. I showed you my sketchbook, remember? Not too many people get to see it."

"That's right. And you're an art student now. I'm proud of you for standing up to your parents about that."

"Speaking of parents, I'm pretty sure your mom hates me. She thinks I'm not good enough for you."

He frowned and shook his head. "Ridiculous. You're the best thing that ever happened to me." Then he winced. "Lame cliché, I know, but it's true."

"I like that lame cliché."

Gage kissed me. I turned into his body, looping my arms around his neck. His mouth searched mine, clinging, sucking lightly at my lips, so gently. He was telling me something with his body, with his lips, and I thought I knew what it was.

But I didn't want to assume.

I plunged my fingers into his soft hair, the strands curling around my fingers. He sighed against my mouth. That sound tugged at me, turned me on and softened my heart just a little more. As if it wasn't soft enough for him already.

He tasted so Gage—of sex and man and everything I loved about him. My pussy warmed, with a hard throb. I felt a trickle of moisture between my legs. This was it for me. He was it. All he had to do was kiss me and I was ready for him.

Our hands explored, slowly, gently, finding all the sensitive spots we'd learned over the past weeks. It felt so good, so damned good. He could take me to sobbing arousal just with his mouth and hands and he did. Over and over, over and over.

"Please," I whispered.

He sat on the bed while I stood in front of him, putting my breasts right at mouth level. He bit lightly at my nipple and I gasped.

"Come on, Gage, please." I reached for his cock.

He moaned as I clasped his hot, hard length in my hand. "Please what?"

"Fuck me."

"God, I love it when you talk dirty." He grinned at me.

I climbed on his lap and straddled him. "Fuck me, Gage."

"Yes, ma'am." He grabbed me around my waist and pulled me down to the bed, rolling me under him.

My legs wrapped around his waist. "You're mine now. I'm not letting you go."

"Good. I don't want to go anywhere." His mouth crashed down on mine, devouring me.

I reached for him again, guiding him into me. We both groaned as he sank deep into my body. My sheath clasped him greedily, hungrily. I rolled my hips upward against him.

"You feel so good," he murmured. He pulled back his hips and thrust again.

I moaned. "So do you."

"You know I could stay inside of you forever."

I grabbed his ass with both hands and shoved my hips up. "I need you. I need this."

He took up a steady, erotic rhythm of thrust and retreat that had me gasping and whimpering within moments. His gaze was fixed on me, blue eyes staring deep into my brown ones, never looking away. I felt as if we were falling together, sinking into each other. Melding.

People talk about a person being their other half. I'd never understood it until that moment. He and I joined together, soul and body, until I couldn't tell anymore which parts were him and which parts were me.

We came together, reached orgasm together. That had never happened to me before. Our bodies shook and trembled against each other, him inside me, my arms and legs wrapped tightly around him, and I knew it didn't matter to me what he did. I didn't care if he stayed here in Avery's Crossing or went back to L.A.; didn't care if he continued acting or quit and became a car salesman. Whatever he did and wherever he went, I would be there with him.

"Nova," he murmured, pressing kisses to my face. "I love you, Nova. I love you."

My eyes stung. I cradled his head in my hands as he continued to cover me with kisses. "I love you too."

"I wasn't supposed to tell you," he whispered. "I don't want to cause you any harm."

"You won't, Gage."

"He might come and get you. It would kill me if anything bad happened to you." He raised his head and stared down at me, his eyes tender and troubled. "But I don't want you to think this is just another fling for me. You're it, Nova. You're the one. I love you."

"I love you too. And I'm not going anywhere."

He gave me a sad smile. "I know. Neither am I."

We were still joined. I didn't want to let him go. I loved feeling him inside me, feeling our bare skin pressed together from chest to toes.

"Does that mean you're going to stay in Avery's Crossing?" I said.

"If you'll have me."

I pressed my lips together. "Of course I'll have you."

"Even if I stop acting?"

"Even if you decide to sell insurance." I kissed his chin. "I love you. Not your job."

"The most important thing to me right now," he said, "is keeping you safe."

"I'll be okay. We have the salt around the house."

He withdrew from my body, making me sigh with regret. "Yeah, but my mom is here. Anything can happen with her around."

I frowned. "You think she'd break the circle on purpose?"

"No, not on purpose." He sighed and shook his head as he gathered me close to him. "I'm probably just being paranoid. She's more terrified of him than anyone."

Chapter 25

Payment Due

Gage:

The shadows in the master bedroom deepened until they were almost so deep I couldn't see anything but the bed where we lay. That was all right. I had everything I needed right here.

The stark, sharply defined black and white looked softer in the low light and so did she.

Nova fell asleep in my arms. I lay there for a while, just watching her. The most boring thing in the world, right? Watching somebody sleep. But it's different when it's someone you love.

I never knew I could feel this way about anyone. The sensations in my body were like nothing I'd ever really experienced—this warm sort of buzzing in my chest, a tightness there too and in my throat. A fullness, like there was too much inside me for my body to contain. I wanted to hold her and protect her forever.

My bladder insisted I get up, though. Reluctantly, I slid my arm out from beneath her slender body and eased myself off the bed. She murmured in a soft voice and rolled over. She must be tired out from all the family craziness and stress. Our parents were doing their best to drive us both nuts. It was getting to me too.

I padded into the bathroom and relieved myself as quietly as I could, so as not to wake her. She deserved to get some rest. I returned to the bed and stood there for a moment, looking down at her. She had dark circles under her eyes.

My hand moved toward her, just to stroke some hair from her forehead. Voices, male and female, came from downstairs—probably Ted and my mom. The sound of the female voice, though, seemed wrong. Too high-pitched and agitated. God. I groaned. Was my mother trying to sneak hard liquor in past Ted again?

I'd told her several times already not to do that. It wasn't fair to Ted to make him choose between keeping his job with me—following my orders to keep booze out of the house—and being nice to my mom.

This was something I had to fix now. She would follow the rules of the house or she'd have to get a hotel room. Or better yet go back to L.A.

I glanced over my shoulder at Nova. Still sleeping peacefully. I smiled at the sight of her snuggled into the bed, her arm around my pillow. I'd take care of this problem with my mother and be right back in bed with my girl in minutes.

Closing the door softly behind me, I walked across the upstairs hall to the stairway, still in my bare feet. The space around me looked as serene as it always did, tastefully decorated and not especially me. But Nova loved it, so it was okay.

Were they still arguing downstairs? For a moment, everything seemed quiet.

Then I heard my mother crying.

I took a deep breath for patience. She was trying the poor-me act again. Sometimes it worked for her, but honestly she was a little old to use that tactic. Sometimes I thought my mom had never really grown up at all.

I ran down the stairs. Their voices were coming from the living room. My mom spoke in a trembling voice. The man answered her, his tones deep and smooth. And he wasn't Ted.

What the fuck? Had she invited a date over?

I blew into the living room. A tall, slim man leaned against the wooden fireplace mantel, smirking at my mother. He had the palest blond hair I'd ever seen on a grown man, almost white. His eyes were pale, too, like crystal or ice. A vague, ancient memory shivered through me, although I didn't know what it meant.

Someone had lit a couple of lamps. Their glow should have given the room a sense of normalcy, but failed. Nothing could be normal with this interloper around.

The dude's clothes were ordinary, just frayed jeans, crisp white running shoes, and a gray hoodie that looked out of place in the elegant room. He looked about my age, maybe a little older. But there was something about him that gave me chills. Real chills, not metaphorical ones. My whole body went icy cold when I looked at him.

It was him. Lucifer. How had I ever thought the black suit guy could be *him?* Now that he stood in front of me, I knew exactly who he was because I remembered that pale hair and those weird, almost-white eyes from before.

Oh, fuck. Oh, fuck, fuck, fuck. What had she done?

"I didn't know," she said, her voice shaking.

"Know what, Ma?" I said, glaring at the pale man.

"Who he was."

"Oh, come now, Nancy," he said, his tone mocking. "You knew exactly who I was."

"No, I didn't. I didn't!"

"Who are you?" I said, advancing on him, my jaw thrust out belligerently.

He smirked again. "Who do you think? Take a guess."

I didn't want to say it. Saying it out loud would make it real. My jaw worked back and forth, my hands clenched and unclenched at my sides, but I couldn't say his name.

Instead, I shot a glare at my mother. "So he just—what? Knocked on the door? And you opened up and invited him in?"

"No! No, I didn't invite him." She shook her head wildly, tears glistening in her eyes.

"You shouldn't lie to your boy, Nancy," he said. "He's bound to find out the truth eventually."

She started crying again. Her mascara ran in black rivers down her cheeks and the strands of her fake eyelashes stuck together in big, spiky clumps.

"How could you let him in here?" I said, my voice rising. "What the hell were you thinking?"

She shook her head again, but didn't answer.

"The salt," I said. "What about the salt?"

Lucifer chuckled. "Salt won't keep out someone like me. The lesser demons, yes, but not me." He turned to my mom. "Nancy, be a dear and let me have some alone time with Gage," he said. "Run along now."

She gulped and wiped the back of her hand across her cheek, smearing the black streaks. "G-gage?"

"Go on, Mom. I'll be fine." I didn't really believe that, but what else could I say? I didn't want anyone else to suffer for me. The fewer people involved in this encounter the better.

"O-okay. Um—okay." She nodded brokenly.

I watched her turn her back on me and walk out of the living room, her shoulders slumped in defeat. She hadn't even tried to defend me. Not that I'd expected her to—I mean, she was the person who made The Deal in the first place. And I didn't want her to fight for me, because there was no way for her to win. Lucifer would eat her alive if it suited him.

But still. To see her turn her back on me like that and leave me to my fate, a fate she had created...

Yeah. Real heart-warming. I'd be sure to get her an extra dozen roses on Mother's Day.

"So, what now?" I growled, turning back to him. "You are the big man downstairs, right?"

He grinned, showing perfect white teeth. "The big man downstairs. That's cute."

"I know, right? It fits you."

"You're a smartass." He pushed off from the mantel. Beneath the hoodie, he wore a white T-shirt with some kind of rock logo on it.

"Let's just get this over with," I said. "No reason to drag it out."

Lucifer shook his head. "Gage, Gage. Haven't you learned anything in all that research you've been doing? I'm not going to take you."

"Why not?"

"Because I can't. At least, not the way you've been thinking."

"Wait a minute," I said, baffled. "You mean the deal is off?"

Lucifer laughed, flashing those perfect teeth again. He could have starred in a tooth-whitening commercial. "I mean there is no deal. There never was. You guessed right, Gage. Your mother had no authority to offer your soul. Only you can do that."

"Then why..." My voice trailed off as I cast around for something that made some kind of sense. Any kind of sense would do. "Why would you tell my mom that the deal was sealed?"

"It amused me. I have to admit it's been a lot of fun watching you and your mom scramble around, scared out of your wits over a deal that was just a figment of your imaginations the whole time."

No. No, I wasn't buying it. There had to be more to the story than a stupid prank.

I took a step toward him. "What about my career?"

"What about it?" He leaned back against the mantel again, crossing his arms over his chest and lounging, clearly still enjoying himself.

"My big break, the rise to fame. Everything happened the way you said it would."

Lucifer shrugged. I couldn't figure out how he could look so completely human and yet so utterly, irredeemably evil at the same time. "I helped you along a bit that first year. After that, it was all you."

I gaped at him. I mean, my mouth actually hung open. "It was all me?"

"Yes, Gage. It was all you."

That didn't compute at all. It couldn't have been me. It was too easy, too smooth. Nobody had it that easy just by chance.

"No. No way." I shook my head. "It couldn't have been."

"Why not? You're highly talented and dedicated. You earned it. You just needed to believe in yourself."

I just needed to believe in myself. Was he going to start spouting New Age style affirmations next?

I glowered at him. "How do I know you're not messing with my mind right now?"

He laughed again, a sound of pure delight. "You don't. But the fact I'm not taking your soul ought to be a clue."

"Fuck." I paced back and forth across the living room. "I can't believe this."

All this time I'd thought I was under the curse of The Deal, and the whole time it was nothing but a hoax. Assuming, of course, that Old Nick was telling the truth now. He watched me with undisguised amusement in those ice-pale eyes, and it made me want to cold-cock the fucker.

Don't ask me why I wasn't pissing my pants at the fact that Satan himself was standing in my living room. Maybe it was because I'd seen him once before, in another much shabbier living room. Or maybe I was just too stupid and angry to be scared.

"The thing is," he said in a mild conversational tone, "once I've been promised a soul, I really prefer to collect. I'm sure you can understand. It doesn't seem fair if a human makes me an offer and I'm unable to collect on that offer."

"Not if it's an offer for something you know you're not entitled to take," I said, giving him a belligerent stare.

He shook his head in mock regret. "I'm sorry to say that part doesn't matter much to me."

"You can't have my soul. I'm using it."

He laughed again. "I like you."

"I'm flattered," I said dryly.

"Now, I could take your mother's soul, since she was the one who initiated the deal. That does seem like a fair and just option. But I don't like it. Her soul is—and I hope I don't offend you by saying this—a bit worn around the edges. Frayed. Deeply stained, as a matter of fact."

"You just said you can't take a soul unless that person offers it. So you're out of luck."

"The soul may be out of my reach. Temporarily, at any rate. But I can take the package that surrounds the soul. It's not something I would ordinarily do, but these are special circumstances."

"The package?" Did he mean what I thought he meant?

"The body, Gage. Try to keep up." He tapped his chin thoughtfully. "So I need a body, with a soul inside, to make up for what I can't have from you, and I'm not enthused about taking your mom. What do you think I should do about that?"

"I don't give a shit." I didn't care what he did, as long as he did it somewhere else.

"Really?" He cocked his head, pale eyes alert with secret amusement. "You have no preference? I can take any soul I like?"

"That's not my decision to make," I said. "You'd probably have to talk to God about that."

Another regretful head shake. "He's so busy these days. He never has time to talk to me. But there is someone I think would make a perfect substitute for you." His pale gaze traveled across the living room toward the hallway. The stairs.

The stairs that led to the second story of the house, where the bedrooms were located. The bedroom where Nova slept.

"No." I started toward him, hand outstretched to grab and detain him. "Not her. Not her!"

My hand closed around his arm. He stared at me, all amusement gone. He had the coldest eyes I'd ever seen.

"The fact that I like you won't stop me from disemboweling you with my bare hands if you annoy me." He peeled off my hand with a grip so strong I could do nothing to resist. "And you're annoying me right now."

"Take me. I want you to take me."

"Ah, but I don't want you anymore. Nova is so much prettier."

I opened my mouth to shout him down. He disappeared before any sound emerged from my throat. I blinked. Glanced around the room.

He was gone.

"Nova!" I tore down the hall and up the stairs, taking them two at a time.

She would be there. She had to be there. Maybe I'd dreamed it all or imagined it.

I pounded down the upstairs hallway and burst through the door of the master bedroom. Flicked on the light. She was gone. The bed was empty, with nothing but rumpled black and white covers to show where she'd been.

"Oh, God. Nova. Nova!"

The bathroom. Maybe she'd gotten up to use the toilet.

I dashed into the bathroom, knowing as I did that it would be empty. And it was. Empty.

I staggered back into the bedroom and fell to my knees beside the bed as an anguished howl tore from my throat.

Nova was gone. He'd taken her.

The End

Breaking Free

Re-unite with Gage and Nova as they overcome the last obstacles dividing them in the haunting final book of the trilogy.

Gage: I never should have told Nova I love her.

When I was ten, my mother sold my soul to the devil in return for my success in Hollywood. Turns out you can't sell someone else's soul. But Lucifer took my girlfriend anyway, as compensation for a deal he never honored in the first place. Now the woman I love is in hell because of me, and I'll do whatever I must to rescue her. Even if I have to go to hell myself to bring her back.

Nova: There's something strange about my new neighborhood. The houses, the apartments, the streets seem so empty. Where are all the people? My only companion, Declan, seems as lost as I feel. And while I like Declan, in my dreams I love a man named Gage. If only he were real...

Tori Minard has published fourteen romance and erotic romance novels and three novellas, in addition to a handful of short stories, both under her own name and as Tessa Tremaine. Her series include The Amaki, Legends Of A Dark Empire, Avery's Crossing, Fortunata: The Jhidris Conspiracy, and Tales Of The Demon Kin.

Tori wrote her first story in elementary school, with a lamentable lack of punctuation. In high school, she spent more time writing fiction than doing homework. Her early stories featured demonic dogs, dolls possessed by evil spirits—no, she'd never heard of Chucky—and politically incorrect post-apocalyptic romance.

She discovered science fiction in the sixth grade, with her dad's recommendation of Edgar Rice Burroughs' At the Earth's Core, the first book in his Pellucidar series. Prior to that, her reading had included ghost stories, animal stories and adventure tales. Around the same time, she was discovering the joys of erotica by sneaking her mom's books and reading all the naughty bits. Her mom claims to have skipped those parts.

After a long detour for such grown-up pursuits as working boring full-time jobs (State of Alaska, U.S. Postal Service), getting married and having a child, she returned to her first love—storytelling. She was born and raised in Alaska, and now lives in the Pacific Northwest with her husband, son, and micro-dog

Discover other titles by Tori Minard

Short Stories:

Stainless Steel Vampire, story number one in the Skye Donovan series
Love Potion Number Ninety, Skye Donovan story number two
If I Should Die; a Legends Of The Dark Empire story
Price of a Rose, a sexy fairy tale (novelette)
Lemon Drop, a sweet erotic toy possessed by a sex spirit

Amaki Novels:

The Heart Moon
Dragon Moon
Blood Moon

Avery's Crossing Novels:

Rush
Bad Company : Book One, The Gage and Nova Trilogy
Bedeviled: Book Two, The Gage and Nova Trilogy
Breaking Free, Book Three, The Gage and Nova Trilogy

Fortunata Novels:

Dirty Magic

Legends Of A Dark Empire Novels:

Temple Of The Heart
Darkness Awakened
Darkness Forbidden
Darkness Beloved
Darkness Embraced

Connect with Tori online

To learn more about Tori, visit her blog at http://www.toriminard.com
Twitter: http://twitter.com/#!/ToriMinard
Facebook: http://www.facebook.com/toriminard.paranormalromance
Pinterest: http://www.pinterest.com/toriminard/

www.ingramcontent.com/pod-product-compliance
Lightning Source LLC
Chambersburg PA
CBHW051944170626
46808CB00007B/2472